The Traitor

The Traitor

a novel by
Dan Sherman

DONALD I. FINE, INC.
New York

Library of Congress Catalogue Card Number: 86-82379

ISBN: 1-55611-000-6
Manufactured in the United States of America
10 9 8 7 6 5 4 3 2 1

This book is printed on acid free paper. The paper in this book meets the guidelines for permanence and durability of the Committee on Production Guidelines for Book Longevity of the Council on Library Resources.

for Steph
with additional thanks
to Lucy and D.J.

The
Low Ground

chapter
one

    On sworn testimony before God and duly appointed officers of the law, a case was established for murder. The facts as recorded were these. On the second day of March, 1780, one Jane Dearborn and one Lt. Colin Smith were found to be dead in a lower Hudson inn commonly known as the White Swan. The victims, unclothed and locked in a fatal embrace, were said to have been en route from New York City where the lieutenant had served with the King's Dragoons. Their intended destination was not determined nor the nature of their journey. The tragic discovery was made by a certain Thomas Finch, a servant indentured at the inn. Immediately following the discovery the youth was found hysterical beneath a staircase, and only after a restorative of rum was he able to tell this story. . .

It had been a Sunday, a dour Sunday with rain and a woodland fog. Since the proprietor, one Samuel Vaughan, had retired to his chambers young Finch had been the first to mark the couple's arrival. A solitary youth of barely sixteen years, it was his habit to pass the afternoons on a window box with a book from his master's shelf. Given his position and the angle of his view, he saw the travelers from quite a long way off. They appeared to be riding in silence with their eyes fixed on the road. Their mounts were clearly exhausted. Their luggage consisted of a beaten portmanteau and a makeshift bundle.

Now given the season and prevailing rumors of the time, at first sight Finch took the travelers to be refugees fleeing from either a British advance or a rebel assault to the south. Then on noting the officer's uniform, he wondered if the pair were not possibly deserters looking for shelter in some neutral cove or inlet. Finally, though, he took them for two more lovers in search of a room to pass the night.

The lieutenant came in first: a tall man in British scarlet. His uniform was damp and soiled from the road. His hair had been bound in a simple knot. After hesitating briefly in the doorway he extended a hand from his cloak. A moment later the woman appeared, also in scarlet.

"Is your master about?" he asked, gray eyes shifting from staircase to doorway.

"About, sir, but indisposed."

"Then perhaps you might fill his station. We are in need of a room." Glancing back to the woman, "And something to eat."

There were three vacant chambers aloft and rather than disturb Mr. Vaughan, Finch led his guests to the far corner room above his own. It was a rude place with three candles on a pewter branch and only feeble light through mullioned windows. The furniture consisted of a narrow truckle bed, two unpadded chairs and a table.

"Should you be requiring a meal from the kitchen, sir, might I suggest—"

"A tray," the lieutenant told him. "A tray from the pantry will be fine."

The woman had still not spoken but her eyes kept meeting the lieutenant's, then falling back to something in the carriage yard below. Finally the lieutenant also went to the window.

"That chaise," he said. "Whom does it belong to?"

"The chaise, sir?"

Tapping a finger to the glass, "Down there."

"Oh, that would be the master Vaughan's, sir."

"And the roan?"

"Also the master's."

Apparently satisfied, he stepped away from the window and took out a coin from his tunic and his eyes seemed to soften. "What do they call you?"

"Thomas Finch, sir."

"Very well, Thomas Finch."

Before shutting the door, a smile may have crossed the woman's face. Her lieutenant, however, had drifted back to the window again.

An hour passed, another dreary Sunday hour. The master had rejoined the household but expressed only a perfunctory interest in the strangers. Like most of the inhabitants along this stretch of the Hudson, Samuel Vaughan had never formally committed himself to either camp in this war. His loyalties were mostly determined by financial considerations, and all that he required of his guests was that they pay in hard currency. As for the rest of the White Swan household, the stranger's presence was hardly even noticed.

It was dusk when Finch returned to the room with a beaten tray from the pantry. Entering, he found the couple seated at the

11

table. A saber had been propped against the wainscot, a pistol laid on the sideboard. Two or three articles of the lady's clothing had been removed from the portmanteau, but the bulk of their luggage had not been touched.

Finch served them in silence: a pint of burnt claret, mutton and peas. Without her cloak and in the candlelight, the woman was more beautiful than the boy had earlier imagined. Her eyes were blue-green. Her hair was very fair. In contrast the lieutenant was a dark man with stony features. Although neither had formally acknowledged Finch's presence they were clearly not purposely ignoring him as was often the habit of passing gentry.

"There's also brandy," Finch said.

The lieutenant shook his head.

"And pudding, although I shouldn't recommend it."

Then suddenly lifting his gaze from the table: "Tell me, Thomas. Are we to be the only guests tonight?"

The woman had also lifted her eyes, waiting for an answer.

"To the best of my knowledge, sir."

"No one from the road?"

"No, sir."

"What about the military patrols?"

"I shouldn't expect anyone on a Sunday, sir."

The evening remained contrary with a wind replacing the mist, driving the rain at a furious angle. Normally after retiring to his room Finch spent at least an hour with his books . . . although a frugal master, Vaughan at least had never begrudged the boy candlelight. On this particular night, though, Finch could not seem to keep his eyes on the page, nor his mind from straying to the chamber above. Now and again he heard the lieutenant's voice, and envisioned the man in black relief against the gabled window. Then hearing the woman's soft response, he imagined her facing the fire with a shawl about her shoulders. He wondered if there were not some plausible excuse he might use to visit them again; to inquire if they wanted breakfast in the morning or assistance with their baggage. He wondered if there were not some practical way he might help; carry a message to friends or stand guard with the officer's saber. And he wondered what he should do if a third stranger appeared and knocked on their door. They seemed to have been concerned about other possible transients.

Perhaps if Finch had been sleeping soundly he might never have awakened at all . . . so soft were the cries against the clattering rain. Then, too, exhausted travelers were often moaning in their sleep, particularly ladies with gentlemen. But after the third or fourth muffled cry he knew that something was amiss. What had previously sounded like the wind was now definitely someone's labored breath.

He climbed the steps slowly, feeling his way. Reaching the landing, he noticed that a window had been left unlatched—a beatable offense. There were also tracks to the doorway.

He hesitated at the door, leaning on the jamb. The only sound was the rain. He thought of retreating and summoning the master, but this was no longer the master's business. Still, he wouldn't have refused the master's flintlock and a firm load of bird shot.

He waited another full minute before knocking—all sound asleep. He knocked again with more conviction—still fast asleep. He tested the knob and watched it slowly turning in his hand. Rather than entering, he let the room draw him in.

The room was very cold. Another window had been left unlatched, and the curtains kept swelling with the breeze. It was also very dark, and at first he could only make out the vague shapes of chairs, bottles on the table and a chamber pot. Then as the curtains slowly parted, filling with the breeze again, he was able to see their faces . . . and all the white limbs entangled on the bed.

He vomited twice on the landing, then again at the foot of the stairs. Unable to call out for assistance, he was later found beating on the walls with his fists.

The Traitor

* * *

According to the coroner's report, submitted by a Dr. Robert John, the victims had died on receiving a cut to the throat, severing the carotid arteries. Thereafter an incision was made to the abdomen, releasing the organs so that they were laid across the left shoulder. The fingers of the right hand were severed, as was the tongue. In spite of a quantity of arterial blood on the walls and ceiling there was no indication of a struggle. Rather it seemed that the murderer had attacked his victims before they were fully roused from sleep. Also of interest was the small quantity of sand and limestone found deposited in their mouths. Although no weapon was discovered, the wounds had apparently been inflicted with an unusually broad and triangular blade, like nothing to be found among local people.

To complement the coroner's report an artist was employed to produce a sketch of the room and adjoining passages. A party of constables was dispatched along the highway, and inquiries were made of local residents. Apart from Thomas Finch, however, no one of the household had anything of substance to say.

For the most part Finch kept to himself through the days that followed, often wandering for hours among the clustered elms that ringed the valley. On occasion hd was found farther afield, almost to the rebel lines. At first these solitary pursuits were seen as a healthy reaction to what he had witnessed, a purgative of sorts, and even Mr. Vaughan was obliged to allow the boy this time to himself. Yet given the depth of the boy's despair, particularly in response to a certain rumor from the south, it soon became clear that young Finch might never recover his senses from that room.

It seemed the rumor originated in New York, and did not reach the White Swan until late March. Up to this time the prevailing theory concerning those murders was that the officer and his lady had been victims of a cruel triangle, and the killer had probably been some jealous spouse or lover. Then simultaneously from

14

several quarters a new and disturbing story began to circulate throughout the valley.

It held that Smith and Dearborn had been spies, rebel spies employed by General Washington. Their career, such as it was, had begun some three years earlier when the lady caught the lieutenant's eye in then British-held Philadelphia. After convincing the man to betray his natural loyalties and throw in his lot with the rebels, she accompanied him back to New York, where they proceeded to steal the British blind in the service of her cause. Although the story offered no particulars about how these spies were undone, the implication seemed clear enough. Smith and Dearborn had not been murdered—they had been executed at His Majesty's request.

Regardless of how others may have reacted to the tale, it seemed little Thomas Finch was never the same again. To begin with, his day-to-day habits changed. He tended to spend much time on solitary chores: mending fences and flagstones in the yard, chopping wood in the evenings. Then although he continued to ramble afield he now went nowhere without his master's squirrel gun. He also abandoned his books in favor of an old pamphlet on musketry.

Another two weeks passed before the proprietor decided that the boy could no longer be ignored. It was now the middle of April, a full month since the murders. That room at the top of the stairs had been stripped. The bedding had been burned. Although not necessarily a patient man, Vaughan had determined to handle the matter with some delicacy. He had even taken care to choose an appropriate time and location: twilight behind the carriage yard, where Finch was often found brooding after a day in the meadows.

Vaughan began casually, leaning beside the boy on a crumbling wall that ringed a potter's field. "My father was a hunter," he said, "although I never saw the point in it myself."

The boy kept on toying with some polished stone he had

collected from the stream. It was an unusually clear day with a view above the dingles to those walnut groves and even beyond to the rebel hills.

"Still, I can't say that I don't enjoy the profit. If you get my meaning."

The boy shrugged. "Only got a hare today."

"A hare, Tommy? A common hare? And all the while I thought it was Redcoats you've been shooting, or Tories at the very least."

A moment passed, the boy appearing spellbound by these formidable hills.

"Listen to me, Tommy. You can't bring them back. What's dead is dead, and those two spies of yours are definitely dead. Best thing now is to put them out of your head. Put them out of your head and let them rest in peace. Do you understand me?"

"Yes, sir."

"And the next time it'll be my birch that does the talking, eh?"

For a while, a day or two, it seemed to Vaughan that the boy was actually beginning to emerge from the shadows that had held him that spring. He gave up the hunt and set himself to regular chores. He also found his appetite again and in the evenings returned to those books he had always cherished.

Then, without warning, he was gone.

He left on a Sunday just after dawn with a makeshift bundle and a squirrel gun. Another hard rain covered his trail, and by the next Friday Vaughan had given up hope of retrieving him. For a time it was rumored that Finch had gone south, where the British were offering hard money to anyone joining His Majesty's ranks. But others maintained that Thomas could not possibly have joined the British, not after what they had done to his guests. No, they said. If little Tommy Finch was anywhere, then he was with General Washington . . . either training for the summer campaigns or for some more immediate form of revenge.

chapter
two

A sense of evil had struck the general public, and so it became
the job of government to see that evil exorcised . . . such, anyway,
was the popular sentiment concerning the White Swan murders.
To a degree this feeling was inspired by a series of Philadelphia
letters drafted in part by Tom Paine. Gossip, a staple of the city,
was everywhere, building the case.

Among those establishments where Philadelphians tended to
gather that spring was a lodging and alehouse popularly called the
Dwarf. It lay on the edge of an untended commons and still
retained a rustic air in spite of the city's encroachment. It was a
modest place, served by a narrow court and a row of dormer
windows. A garden in the rear had all but gone to ruin and there

was almost always standing water in the yard. Still, the walls
were of stout brick set with black headers and the rooms were
reasonably clean with only the occasional rat.

The original proprietor had been a William Dunn, but on his
death at Germantown the place had passed into the care of an
uncle named Drapier. Dunn's fourteen-year-old daughter still
lived there, as did the ghost of her mother (or so it was said).
There were also a cook and boy to help with menial chores, while
young Sarah Dunn served as chambermaid.

In the main, patrons of the Dwarf were local clerks and
shopkeepers. Owing to the late Mr. Dunn's patriotic reputation, a number of military officers also drank here in the evenings. Consequently talk was usually of a political nature and
generally considered reliable. When rumors of the White Swan
murders, for example, began spreading throughout the city the
Dwarf became one of the few relatively dependable sources of
information.

At the outset talk of the murders centered on the more gruesome details. Following a public description of the bodies as
discovered by young Finch, it seemed that everyone began to
speculate on the nature of the weapon. There was also speculation
about what sort of monster could have committed such a crime,
and what form of British beast could have sanctioned it. Concur-
rently there was discussion about the victims, and a number of
residents claimed to have known them from the summer of '78.

But the most talked-about subject of the season was Washington's expected reprisal. Although not said to have been a vindic-
tive man, His Excellency could not let the deaths go unrevenged.
After all, it was one thing to catch and hang spies, quite another
to gut them like pigs.

For a while the consensus in the Dwarf and elsewhere was that
Washington's retaliation would be swift and direct. The capture
of two Tory spies seemed fitting, perhaps even an assassination.
Keener minds held that the general would never rest until the

specifically guilty party was found. Which meant there would be an investigation, a discreet investigation conducted by a gentleman with experience in these affairs.

As predicted he arrived on a Thursday. By chance, or coincidence, the first to see him was the proprietor's young niece, Miss Sarah Dunn. Although he must have come by coach, Sarah at first heard nothing except the clap of his boot heels. He was a lean figure of medium height. He wore a blue cloak in the military fashion, light jackboots and a riding frock.

When he took off his hat she saw that his hair had been naturally cropped, as if permanently windblown. His waistcoat and breeches were also military but without any distinction. She supposed he was about twenty-five.

Her next impression came from a conversation overheard on the staircase. The stranger had entered the parlor, where he was received by the proprietor. Although amiable enough to regular patrons, George Drapier was a hard man with a talent for small acts of cruelty. He had even been known to take advantage of the odd traveler for no other reason than his own amusement. Yet faced with this particular stranger, he soon became uncommonly polite. The stranger remained distant, with a soft but commanding voice. He explained that from time to time he would be receiving deliveries and that these were not to be tampered with. He was also to be informed of anyone taking an interest in his presence, anyone at all.

Before presenting herself to the stranger, Sarah returned to her room to take care of her appearance. Although quite beautiful with flaxen hair and pale blue eyes, she was said to have been a dull child. She also lacked piety, according to Drapier. She sensed that this stranger might forgive her these faults, perhaps overlook them . . . after all, he was a man who had so easily frightened her uncle.

It was nearing four o'clock when she finally met the stranger.

19

The Traitor

She had entered his room with a basin of water and found him facing the window. He still wore the cloak and boots but his gloves had been tossed to the mantle. Candles had been lit on a sconce by the door, three more burned in a pewter branch.

"Not to be disturbing you, sir, but I'm to inquire about your supper?"

There was also a brace of pistols on the table, and a curiously thin dagger.

"My supper?" he said in a flat voice, without so much as a glance to her.

"Yes, sir. To inquire whether you'll be wanting it downstairs or in—"

Suddenly turning to face her: "I think just a cold plate here will do, thank you."

"A cold plate, sir?"

"With wine if you've got it."

"Very well, sir. And your breakfast in the morning?"

He turned to the window again. "It doesn't matter."

By rights she should have left him then, retreating with a differential nod. But something in his posture held her, fixed her to the floor.

"By the way, you're the niece, aren't you?"

"Sir?"

"Drapier is your uncle."

"Yes, sir. He is."

"And your name is Sarah?"

"Yes, sir."

"Well, you can tell them that mine is Matty Grove . . . in case they were wondering."

Later that evening, with the arrival of his luggage, she was able to fix a title to the name he had given her: Lieutenant Colonel. Beyond this nothing was certain.

By morning it seemed that this Matty Grove had become a

splendid mystery—evoking rumors everywhere and leaving a number of citizens uneasy. Of his personal habits, Sarah was able to determine only that he was fond of madeira and had difficulty sleeping. Apart from his weapons and a miniature of a woman in enamel, his possessions were of little interest. Indeed, she found only one clue about the nature of his mission: a neatly bound sheaf of letters and newspaper articles devoted to those White Swan murders.

She mainly saw him in the mornings when she would enter his room at about seven to find him half-reclining in a chair by the unlatched window. In buckskin and a blouse with rounded cuffs, he looked, she thought, vaguely like a buccaneer. Sometimes she found him toying with that dagger, testing the point on the woodwork. Although at first he never engaged her in conversation, they always exchanged civilities. Then by degrees he actually started to talk to her.

"That printer," he would say, referring to a gentleman he had seen in the tavern below, "is he often about?"

"Often enough, sir."

"And that friend of your uncle's," referring to a certain Mr. Hatch, "also a regular customer?"

"Regular enough."

"What do you know of them?"

"Nothing more than I've seen."

"But you've heard them talking from time to time."

"Yes . . ."

"So then what do you figure they're made of?"

She was startled by the directness of his question, but said nothing, only shook her head.

Another time he asked about the prevailing gossip concerning those awful murders. Who was believed to be the guilty party? How did they account for the act? To what did they attribute the method of execution . . . and what was their opinion of their investigator?

"I presume they would have had Washington send them an entire brigade."

"No, sir, not exactly . . ."

"Then what?"

It seemed that whenever he questioned her with some intensity that dagger found its way into his hands again.

"It's only idle talk, sir."

"What sort of talk? That bats are in the belfry? That the person's in league with the devil?"

"That you once had a wife and child in the west country, but the Redcoats induced the Indians there to murder them, and after that you collected scalps to show on your belt."

He was silent for a moment. "That's not the whole truth, Sarah."

"I knew it wasn't."

"I never actually showed the scalps on my belt."

Eventually he asked about her, her memories of her father, her relationship with Drapier.

"I lived with an uncle once myself," he told her. "A schoolmaster. Although I can't say he taught me anything beyond the futility of the rod. Does yours beat you?"

"No, sir."

"Never?"

"No."

"I bet he does. I bet he does it whenever it strikes his fancy." Then with a smile she had never seen before, "Still, it's one thing to suffer a beating and another to submit to it. If you get my point."

Of his own existence he told her little more, so she was obliged to rely on the word of others. Which said that he had originally hailed from Boston but had never cottoned to city life. Also that he had fought an irregular war in some secret capacity . . . he was a master of spies, or a master at catching spies. The fact that he wore a wedding band and had an enamel miniature of a woman

22

lent further credence to that story about the murder of his wife
and child; and if that was true, then it only stood to reason that
he must have viewed this war as a highly personal affair.

Among the rest of the household and patrons of the Dwarf the
view of Mr. Matty Grove was not so compassionate. Granted
there were those who believed he was precisely the sort of man
one would call on to deal with a British outrage, but there was
also the feeling that the cure could prove worse than the ailment.

At the forefront of these early critics was the Dwarf's own
George Drapier. Although Drapier would say he had not liked
the stranger from the start, it was an incident from the sixth day
that especially disturbed him. Worse, it involved the child and so
had the potential for sin. It happened on a Wednesday at about
eight in the evening. Conspicuously negligent since the stranger's
arrival, Sarah Dunn had finally proved herself insolent as well.

Traditionally punishments were meted out in the stables,
where a birch was kept for that purpose. On this particular
occasion, however, Drapier felt that the lesson would be better
learned in the counting room. There was a low stool to accommodate the child, and the walls were sufficient to muffle her cries
while still leaving certain guests impressed. So the child was
summoned from the kitchen and told to report to the counting
room.

Drapier had positioned himself in the corridor to wait for her.
Although he kept the birch concealed behind his back she guessed
what lay in store the moment she rounded the corner. She did not,
however, seem particularly concerned. Could she have sensed
that the stranger would appear on her behalf?

As it was, he did appear out of nowhere just as she approached
the door. It was impossible to tell what had alerted him, whether
an overheard word or some subtler sign. Either way he appeared
very suddenly on the landing above. His gaze was fixed, implaca-
ble, and for some time no one seemed able to move. Then although

nothing was said, the message was plain enough: if anyone was to
be punished in this city, the stranger himself would see to it.

That this Matty Grove was a dangerous and temperamental
man soon became established in everyone's mind. If nothing else
he was known to have been an Indian fighter, a desperate occupation. It was further known that he had served with bloody distinction on at least two occasions against the British, and was still a
name to them. His pistols were of a uniquely professional design
with a threaded plug to facilitate loading and to insulate the
charge, and the dagger was also of a particularly gruesome design.

So armed and obviously determined, few doubted Grove's potential for dealing with these White Swan murders. Rather it was
his method that concerned them, along with his grim manner.
The problem was perhaps most succinctly stated by Jameson
Hatch one evening in conversation at the Dwarf. An attorney by
trade, Hatch had always prided himself on having a penetrating
mind. He was also frequently unemployed, which left him plenty
of time to meddle in the affairs of others.

Yet to his credit Hatch's analysis of the stranger's progress did
rest on a fair bit of logic. "Given that the man has been charged
with the investigation of a monstrous British crime," he argued,
"why then does he not seek the guilty party on British ground?"

"Because he's a fool," Drapier shouted. "A fool and, no doubt,
a coward at heart."

"No, not a fool," Hatch said, "and definitely not a coward.
Rather I put it to you thus: our Mr. Matty Grove does not seek
the murderer on British ground because the murderer is not on
British ground. He is on our ground . . . *somewhere among us
even as I speak to you now.*"

After this pronouncement, there was clearly a change. Grove
could come and go as before but suddenly the gossip stopped. A
windless chill held the spring in check. It seemed the whole city
was content to let the man work in silence.

chapter
three

The investigation of the White Swan murders began on the first day of June. Grove had gotten up with the milk carts and a faint tune from a tin whistle in the lane below. The sky was flat gray, odors from a tanning yard hung in the breeze. Sarah had left a porringer of hot water-gruel at the door but he couldn't face it. There was also a copy of a local gazette that she must have supposed would interest him. It told of a skirmish between New York militia and a detachment of His Majesty's horse. At least thirty-five men fell to bayonet, saber and musket shot. There were also two more column inches devoted to those murders, but nothing that had not been reported before.

Although at first it might have seemed that Matty Grove was

indifferent to these murders, this was not true. Indeed, the death of Smith and Dearborn struck at the very heart of his professional sensibilities—the man was indeed a master of spies, or what might be called an intelligence officer. His career had begun three years earlier around the port of Boston. From Boston he had followed the ebb and flow of this conflict to New York and Long Island, Pennsylvania and the Jerseys. It was also true that his family had fallen victim to an Indian raid the British had precipitated, and thereafter the war had become a highly personal matter.

Beyond this sketchy history of the man there was little to say. Those who knew him well knew him as a quiet man. He had no close friends, as far as anyone could tell, and was not said to have a woman.

His entrance into this case had begun with a letter received on thirteenth of May. En route from New England he had witnessed the execution of a Tory, possibly a spy. His accommodations were a bit more expensive than he had anticipated but all in all seemed fitting enough. Indeed, he had always envisioned ending this war in a narrow room, hearing only the news that flies brought. The view, too, was almost comforting: an alley littered with vegetable stalks, then half a mile of blackened rooftops to a nest of rigging above the harbor. Were it not for the child he might have believed himself dead.

He did not see the child the morning that it all began. There was only a lame boy in the yard to tend his horse and peddlers at the gate as he slipped through the back lanes. He rode with a slack rein and a slight stoop until the horse, after four days' confinement, seemed content to pick up the pace. Here and there a curtain parted and a face appeared in a window. The shops, however, were still tightly shuttered and the alleys were empty.

The meadow lay about five miles beyond the city, a quiet circle of high grass filled with dogwood and dwarfed willows. A creek fed from higher streams ran a haphazard course to a mill. Trees, mostly oak and walnut, grew along the lower slopes. Although no fighting had ever disturbed this particular meadow it would seem to be a fitting place for the start of this affair. A spy, employed against the British only three years before, had been shot and killed not far from this spot. Another had been hanged just a mile to the south.

On arriving at the meadow, Grove was met by the sound of birds and the echo of a distant axe. Then two horsemen appeared from between the darker oaks. The first, if the uniform could be believed, was a corporal from one of the lower Pennsylvania regiments. Behind him and somewhat closer to the trees rode a young colonel. As the parties drew closer, the colonel slowly raised an arm in half salute. Grove's acknowledgement was barely perceptible, a brief nod before dismounting. Still closer, the colonel shouted Grove's name. Grove's half-whispered response, however, could not possibly have been heard: *Tallmadge.*

Benjamin Tallmadge was a sober man with a boyish face. Not quite twenty-six at the outset of these inquiries, he was typical of officers at Washington's side and a reminder that the revolution was still a struggle of youth. He and Grove had originally met in Setauket, where Tallmadge had spent three weeks forging a chain of agents into New York City. Grove had been enlisted to deal with a particularly troublesome British lieutenant, which ultimately proved to be a murderous task. Yet whenever he thought about Benjamin Tallmadge, he tended to recall a soft-spoken voice in a chilly landscape.

There was much to remind one of that murderous season now: an unusual cold that seemed to rise from the earth, the cries of unseen crows, odors of leaf mold and damp grass. Even the corporal seemed vaguely familiar from some diaster at White Plains or Long Island. Yet if Tallmadge had then been an unshakable force, here he seemed only marginally composed. Grove had accompanied the man along a deer path to the edge of the stream, where he finally seemed to sag into the grass. A flask

27

punctured by bayonet at Bunker Hill lay between them on the moss. Willows collected at random would help keep the mosquitoes at bay.

"You never actually met them, did you?" Tallmadge began. "Smith and Dearborn, I mean."

"No."

"Pity, since I think you would have found them charming . . . particularly the seamstress."

Birds, which had first fled at the sound of human voices, were now gradually returning. Otherwise it was dead still.

"Then you never doubted their loyalty?"

"Of course not."

"Their intentions?"

"They were in love, Matty. They were deeply in love with one another, and rather deeply in love with this Revolution. Anyway, the proof was in the pudding. Their submissions were flawless, veritable gold."

"So then what happened?"

"They were murdered. Butchered, to be precise. The throats cut. The entrails rather artfully removed."

"With some clear method in mind?"

"So it would appear."

"As if to discourage others?"

"Perhaps."

"Then what's the point?"

They began to walk randomly, following the deer path deeper into the trees. Had they continued far enough they would eventually have come to a high glen where two more unlikely lovers were said to have been murdered. Perhaps by a jealous suitor. Their names had been forgotten, but apparently their ghosts still lingered among the pines, presumably waiting for someone like Grove to avenge their deaths as well.

"The point is this," Tallmadge continued once they had paused again, "the British were not directly involved. Smith and

Dearborn were in our employ as confidential agents, but they were not murdered by the British."

"Yes?"

"They were betrayed. They were betrayed by someone within *our* camp . . . presumably because they were much too close to a rather foul secret."

"Is that Washington's theory?"

"*And* mine. Listen to me, Matty. I saw to their security myself. And it was tight, tight as a drum."

"How was the correspondence maintained?"

"Dispatches were buried in the commons, then collected by courier and ferried across the sound."

"And the courier knew them?"

"Neither by name nor sight."

"What identified the dispatches?"

"A code of my own invention and a sympathetic stain."

"And the replies?"

"The same."

They had settled again on a pair of moss-bound stumps. A pool, seemingly bottomless, lay below. There was also quite a long view of the city, especially its steeples.

"Admittedly I do not have your mind for this," Tallmadge said, "but if you'll only hear me out—"

"I've said nothing, Benjamin."

"Then mark it. The last letters from Smith and the woman described a thing we've not seen before—a link, an undisclosed link between someone in our camp and someone within the British camp. Now, this link appears to have been maintained at great expense to the Crown but was justified by the quality of intelligence it brought . . . intelligence plucked directly from our innermost chambers. Enough?"

But Grove merely continued toying with a leaf. "There are those who will tell you that the British have placed spies beneath every bed in Philadelphia, particularly congressional beds."

The Traitor

"But we are not discussing spies, Matty. We are discussing a traitor, a traitor of no small consequence. An officer, perhaps even a general. And when he discovered that my lieutenant and the woman were on to his scent, he employed some beast to butcher them . . . obviously as a warning to others."

"And this is also Washington's theory?"

"It's a postulate, but certainly the facts suggest it convincingly."

"And how did your Smith and Dearborn supposedly stumble on this postulated traitor?"

"Shortly after their arrival in New York Smith received a posting to Clinton's office. Primarily his duties were clerical, but now and again he was charged with the copying of certain letters . . . letters of a confidential nature."

"Letters to whom?"

"Undisclosed, but the subject was plain enough—the maintenance and security of a special source of information."

"And where were these letters to be sent?"

"London."

A wind had risen, a warm wind from the west that was said to have prompted camp fever. As this point, however, Tallmadge had grown quite cold and rather resembled a clerk or teacher out of his element.

"It's a matter of logic," he went on. "Smith and Dearborn discover evidence of a traitor within our midst. That evidence is forwarded by me through usual channels, and within the month the both of them are dead . . . worse than dead, if one considers what was actually done."

"What do we know of the killer himself?"

"Not a great deal. His Excellency seems to feel that the beast was African. Others hold that he was Indian. Either way, he's not my primary concern. I want the one that held the purse."

"Still, I may have to start with the killer."

30

"Suit yourself."

"And I shall need whatever exists in the way of records."

"Of course."

"And, Benjamin . . . keep the Congress out of it. They'll only get in my way."

Having finally risen again, they slowly made their way along the path. Although any number of trees might have served the hangman, the last oak before the meadow seemed particularly appropriate. It was not a large thing, but the branches were high and firm.

"Incidentally," Tallmadge said suddenly, "should you want to speak with that courier, his name is John Clock."

"One-legged Clock?"

"Yes."

"What sort of a choice was that?"

"A poor one, I suppose. At any rate you'll find him in the Highlands. And Matty? Do bear in mind that this war is no longer quite what it seems."

"Was it ever?"

Tallmadge shook his head. I don't know. I only know that it's gotten filled with all sorts of conflicting forces. Generals flirting with speculators. Congressmen flirting with stock-jobbers. Meanwhile, the poor soldiers in the field are dying for want of bandages."

Grove turned to face the man, saying nothing.

"It's not a joke, Matty. There are those who fear mutiny."

"So they should fear it."

Tallmadge paused again, eyes still fixed on that formidable oak. "Let me put it another way. This White Swan business is a very different matter than anything we've seen before. It suggests something very rotten, something rotten at the core. Need I say it again? There seems to be something decidedly rotten somewhere in the core of this Revolution, *and it must be cut out.*"

31

The Traitor

* * *

Having now arrived at where they had started, the conversation took a somewhat more personal turn—a few finishing words while waiting for the corporal with their mounts.

"It hardly inspires you at all anymore, does it?" Tallmadge said softly.

There were once again rainclouds to the west, and the whine of those bagpipes from still farther afield.

"What do you mean?" Although it was obvious now. This was to be a season of those pipes, and still another year for the hangman.

"This war, this Revolution. I suspect that it no longer touches you."

Grove ran the back of his hand across his mouth. "I'll find your traitor, Benjamin . . . if that's what concerns you."

"Oh, I'm not questioning your professional talents. I just should hate to think you've lost sight of the larger vision. Very well, the savages murdered your family. There's still a life, if you want it." He glanced at his feet, then at Grove's profile. "Do you realize that we can win this war?"

"The French will win it."

"Same thing, so long as they're on our side. And once the British have been booted into the sea we shall possess the richest continent in the world?"

"And the Spanish?"

"A moot point. The real question is who among us shall govern? I suppose you've heard that Congress is split into more parts than anyone can count. You might also stay away from the Gates circle. I no longer trust them."

The corporal appeared, leading Grove's mount. A black valise containing what would form the basis of the White Swan file had been attached to the saddle.

"And while you're at it," Tallmadge added, "you might further bear in mind the public sentiment. Although they want justice done, they become uneasy when it's administered too close to home, if you get my drift."

Grove nodded, lifting himself to the saddle. "I'm a soldier, Benjamin. Politics are not my province."

"Just the same, bear it in mind. Anyway, you're not a soldier either . . . you're a hunter."

On leaving, Grove heard Tallmadge call out to him some further warning about the rain and road. In fact the rain did not actually fall until dusk. Then it came suddenly in furious sheets from the west, and although the bridges held, the lower lanes were soon awash.

It was close to midnight when Grove finally returned to the Dwarf. Although lanterns had been extinguished for hours the fires still glowed in the grates. The rain had stopped, however, so that there was only the ticking of wet leaves. Sarah Dunn heard him first on the landing, then again like a cat in the corridor. Although she had contemplated leaving her door ajar she decided that all it would invite was another brief glimpse of his shadow.

In a sense Sarah's own conception of these first steps were only slightly less defined than Grove's. Having learned that the man had spent the day with one of Washington's officers, she had guessed that the overture had ended, and to that extent she was frightened. In market stalls on the High Street citizens still may have pondered Matty Grove's mysterious past, but in fact the past was behind him, and the future would be like nothing anyone imagined.

On entering his chambers he was silent, and for a while she thought he was asleep. Then came the rhythmical tread of his heels on the floorboards, back and forth across from wall to wall. Next she heard what might have been the sound of leaves in the wind, or perhaps rustling papers. A bright child, Sarah, contrary to the prevailing wisdom. Then it was very quiet.

The hunt had begun.

chapter
four

It was late when Grove finally set his mind to it, at least two
in the morning if the chimes from below could be trusted. He was
not particularly tired, however, and the night sounds seemed
appropriate enough, even comforting: restless pigeons stirring in
the eaves, the distant clatter of a solitary dray, mice behind the
plaster. Someone, presumably the child, had even left a bottle of
madeira, a wedge of cheddar and an apple—not an extravagant
meal, but certainly more than one might expect at the White
Swan.

There were seven individual packets of notes relating to this
White Swan affair. Some, Grove found, had been carefully sealed
in oilskin. The remainder had been tied with ribbon. The packets

were in no particular order, and Grove spent a long time arranging them chronologically. Next he laid out his tools: ink and quill, light and sconce, a quantity of paper bound to the quarto. Although the madeira was still close at hand, he did not immediately touch it.

Specifically, the first reference to the affair was a letter: Tallmadge to His Excellency on the first of the year, 1778. Although cryptic in many respects, the gist seemed plain enough in hindsight. Jane Dearborn had been a fairly new link to the Philadelphia chain, while Colin Smith had merely been one more British officer she had managed to ensnare through the course of a frivolous season. By way of background, Tallmadge had noted that Miss Dearborn was essentially a modest girl, child to a miller, niece to a constable. She was described as an uncommonly pretty woman with a look that one associated with "country girls." Supposedly she had lost a brother at Concord, which more or less accounted for her dedication to this cause. On the other hand, Smith was described as a plain but honest fellow from Somersetshire. At the outset their meeting and subsequent relationship had probably not attracted attention. Yet when it became clear that the lieutenant's affections for this woman had actually supplanted his loyalty to the Crown, the game grew altogether more engaging.

Although Tallmadge had included several notes in an effort to chronicle Miss Dearborn's progress through this period, nothing seemed quite so succinct as Grove's personal memories of the season: a certain harsh Tuesday in November where the army lay in shambles on a windswept hill. Congress had been standing uncomfortably in Baltimore while the British sneered from the Capitol. There had been rumors of plague, and isolated instances of starvation. Yet despite it all, Tallmadge remained optimistic with his Smith and Dearborn affair.

"Imagine them as a pair of lice . . . a pair of lice attached to the British body," he had told Grove at the time.

35

"How do you intend to direct them?" Which had been a reasonable enough question given the demands on Ben Tallmadge's time.

"With exceptional care."

"Yourself?"

"If need be."

The man's letters to Washington had been no less enthusiastic: "This lieutenant is one of Howe's own pups. He suckles from the same teat as the rest of them."

A month had passed, still another dreadful month with the army on the verge of mutiny and Congress hamstrung by a pack of merchants. It was also a time of rampant jealousy with at least one obvious attempt to supplant Washington with Gates. Yet Tallmadge continued to remain undaunted, with three impressive submissions from his cherished Smith and Dearborn. "As you can plainly see," he boldly noted in the margin of the first, "we at last have a finger on the British pulse."

The record contained only fragments of Smith and Dearborn's existence following the British abandonment of Philadelphia and return to New York City. Apparently the couple had been among the first to leave, just ahead of the British army. Precisely how Smith had then managed to obtain a posting with General Clinton's staff was not explained, nor how Dearborn continued to slip away for periodic meetings with Tallmadge. Their efforts, however, had never been more appreciated, which was ultimately part of the reason why Tallmadge grew exceedingly nervous as time went on.

In all Tallmadge had included three dispatches from Smith and Dearborn's last weeks in New York City: eighteen transcribed pages tied with another bit of tattered ribbon. After struggling with the knot for a minute or two Grove withdrew a pocketknife. Although the night should have been temperate with a summer breeze, the chill had returned.

Evidently the woman had drafted the majority of these latter reports, although now and again the lieutenant's voice was also quite clear: "Dined in quarters with John André and others from Clinton's staff. Talk of little consequence until a certain Mr. Anderson remarked that the capons had a distinctly rebel flavor. (Capons in a wine sauce). This prompted several more wry comments, and a further comment that cannot be taken in jest given recent intelligence received."

At the heart of the matter lay what Tallmadge would call "an unseemly alliance between persons in Philadelphia and others in New York City." At the outset this alliance appeared to have been financially based, and involved the trade of foodstuffs and timber for which the British paid dearly. Yet in time it became clear that the material trade was only incidental to an altogether more devious sale of military secrets.

"It would seem that the enemy has managed to cultivate an agent among us," Tallmadge wrote Washington, "an agent of some tact and station." In order to support the claim he offered no less than seven instances wherein British generals appeared to have had an uncanny foreknowledge of American movements. There were also the various references to the matter found in Clinton's personal correspondence as reported by Smith, and further corroboration in fragments of London-bound packets.

To his credit, Washington's immediate concern had been for the physical safety of his spies. "Surely new measures must be taken to insure that the couple is not betrayed by the traitor they seek." Whether or not such measures were taken was not evident from the record, but it was clear that the danger was gradually increasing. "Be advised," Dearborn wrote, "we are not on the scent of an ordinary British agent, but rather a kind of Hydra ... which is to say that the subject is a persistent evil with a finger in many pies." Additionally Smith noted that the traitor's postulated link with the British was an exceedingly complex affair, possibly involving dozens of unwitting subordinates between Philadelphia and New York City.

The Traitor

Apparently there had been an interview at this juncture, another brief and clandestine meeting between Tallmadge and the woman along the Hudson.

"Is it possible," Tallmadge had asked the seamstress, "that Clinton is himself an agent in this affair?"

"Possible and even likely," the woman had responded.

"An agent for powers in London?"

"It would seem so, yes."

"Which would then make our traitor a man of international relationships?"

"Yes."

There was a point just before the end when Smith and Dearborn believed themselves to be close to the beast. "Having laid aside all previous notions and looked at the thing afresh," Tallmadge reported to Washington, "it would appear that our quarry must possess at least these traits. He is traveled and thus internationally known. He is not without local influence and resources in the military. His reputation precedes him in a number of quarters, for he is generally held to be a father of this Revolution."

Attached to the same message, Tallmadge had further submitted a list: twenty-three names of those whom he could not place above suspicion. The names appeared in alphabetical order beginning with John Adams and ending with Artemus Ward. Some were followed by brief notations regarding their standing in Congress or the army. Others like Hancock, Jefferson and Alexander Hamilton needed no explanation at all.

There were eight pages in the last packet, but Grove knew that they specifically concerned the murder, and so laid them aside for the moment. Although not yet formally dawn, the harbor lights had faded and a sloop had dropped her sails. There were also frigates running for the high sea, and a coaster in the bay. The streets had begun to stir with the cries of teamsters and reluctant horses. From below, however, there were still no sounds except for the child's tread in the pasageway.

He unlatched the door to admit her, then returned to the dregs of madeira—an entire bottle consumed without even recalling the first glass. The candles, too, were spent, while the floor was littered with the night's debris: wadded bits of paper, plugs of tobacco and burnt cork. The window panes were smeared with fingerprints, but the child seemed not to notice any of it.

She entered slowly, hesitating briefly in the doorway. If at times she was quite clearly still a girl, there were also moments when she was virtually a woman. Her hair, unbound, lay about her shoulders. Her dress, gathered at the waist, did not quite conceal that her feet were bare. Although she had murmured something about fetching his breakfast, it seemed that she was concerned about him, his welfare.

"What's the hour?" he asked.

She shook her head. "Just past five, I should think."

"And the household still asleep?"

"Yes, sir."

He laid down the bottle and returned to the window. What had earlier resembled a wolf was merely a dog prowling through the lane below. "Still asleep and dreaming?"

"Sir?"

"Dreaming about another bloody murder?"

"No, sir."

He ran a hand across his eyes and supposed that he was at least a little drunk. "When does your uncle rise?"

"Shortly."

"And the others?"

"About the same."

"Well, see if you can't keep them quiet."

"Yes, sir."

The Traitor

He caught another glimpse of her sympathetic gaze in the glass and realized that he must have looked terrible. "I understand they're now saying that our murderer was a demon, a demon with unnatural powers. Do you believe it?"

"I'm sorry, sir?"

"Do you believe that the killer was a demon, Sarah?"

She hesitated again, still watching his reflection in the glass. "I shouldn't pay attention to anything that comes from gossip, sir."

"Even if it may contain a shred of truth?"

She left him at the table again, the last packet still fixed with His Excellency's seal. The fire had died in the grate again. He supposed that he should have asked her for coffee, and further that the wine had been a mistake. Indeed, the late lieutenant and his seamstress might not have slept so soundly had they stayed clear of the wine . . .

Tallmadge had obviously spent a fair amount of time attempting to reconstruct his agents' last days, but finally was able only to establish the barest sequence of events. Apparently the first indication that all was not well came on a Thursday. Details were still vague but obviously something had terrified the lieutenant, and by Saturday he and the woman had fled. Fresh mounts had been provided by a sympathetic blacksmith. Their first meal on the road had consisted of a threepenny loaf, pork and beer. The White Swan had probably been an arbitrary choice, mostly determined by the storm.

The last notes, of course, were meager. Having dined on cold plates from the larder, the couple had retired early. A scullery maid recalled seeing no light in the window past eight o'clock. Nor were there voices heard past nine. Despite the cold their clothing had been discarded and laid across the chairs. They had then either copulated, or else merely clung to one another . . . in desperation? Finally, obviously exhausted from the road, they had slept. The lieutenant's pistol, loaded and primed, had been left an arm's length away. The saber, propped against the skirting board, had been equally accessible.

So then what had occurred?

The question seemed implicit in every drop of ink that followed: what could have possibly happened?

There were fragments of three depositions taken from local residents. Although of no definite value there seemed to be one exchange that could not be ignored. The deponent had been an itinerant peddler by the name of Jack Match. His age was given as thirty-seven years. His role in the affair was that of a passive witness. On the night of the murder he claimed to have been sleeping some two miles south of the inn beneath a ruined cart. Yet on waking to the sound of hoofbeats, he left his bed (such as it was), and crept through the tall grass to the edge of the highway.

> *Q. And at approximately what hour was this?*
> *A. Late. Midnight at the earliest.*
> *Q. And you maintain that a horseman appeared?*
> *A. Or the devil astride a horse.*
> *Q. At what distance?*
> *A. Close enough.*
> *Q. To see his face?*
> *A. Not his face, but his aspect.*
> *Q. Which was?*
> *A. Black, black as the night.*
> *Q. And his size?*
> *A. As big a man as any you'd care to meet. And with an odor about him.*
> *Q. An odor?*
> *A. Even from a dozen paces you could smell it— sweet, like burning flesh.*
> *Q. And you saw him then ride to the inn?*

The Traitor

A.   Not all the way, but in that general direction.
Q.   And then?
A.   And then nothing, since I wasn't about to ask his
       business nor tag along for the ride.

There were sketches attached of the carriage yard and passage-ways, the landings and staircase. Further details regarding the proximity of an oak in the garden and the window through which the murderer had entered had also been noted below.

Yet what then could have happened?

Undoubtedly on unfamiliar gound, the killer must have moved with some caution. The clatter of rain may have been a comfort, but the moonlight must have been thin. Nor could he have been certain that the innkeeper kept no dogs. The tool he had used to disengage the latch was still a matter of speculation, but there-after his steps seemed obvious enough.

The room had been darker than the passageway, and the killer must have paused until his eyes had become accustomed to it. The lieutenant had been sleeping closest to the door, the seamstress beside him. Possibly confident that his footsteps would not be heard above the storm, the intruder may have moved quickly. Then again he may have hesitated, testing the water, as it were.

Although Tallmadge had devoted considerable thought to the last details, he had been left with little more than shadows. His notes, like the tracks of insects in the margin, were posed as questions: What meaning the severed fingers and tongues? Why the intestines laid on the shoulders? What significance the sand and limestone? The imprint of a hand in blood on the wall suggested that the killer had actually straddled the bodies in order to perform the crime; while additional prints on the ankles and wrists suggested that there had been much handling and adjust-ment of the limbs. Although there was no evidence of sexual violation there were clear hints of a certain intimacy: the arrange-ment of the hair on the pillows, the arms above the head, the

interlocking fingers of the left hand. Yet even savages, Tallmadge had concluded, were not normally known to engage in
such business unless driven to a tribal frenzy. "Thus it would
seem that this is surely not something from our era," he wrote,
"but rather something from an altogether different century."

It was midmorning when Grove laid the last pages aside; the
household awake, the streets alive again. On rising from the table
in search of his boots he caught sight of a mouse beneath the
wainscot. He did not feel like killing it.

He found the child kneeling at the bottom of the staircase,
apparently engaged in dusting. Her left cheek was faintly discolored, and he guessed that the proprietor had struck her again—
backhanded, full force. Her eyes, however, showed no trace of
tears.

She said something about his breakfast as he drew closer, but
he ignored her and knelt down. Then lightly tracing the outline
of the bruised cheek: "I wonder if you might do me a small favor,
Sarah?"

"A favor, sir?" Her voice was also soft, hardly more than a
whisper.

"I should like you to keep a watch on my room today. Do you
think you can manage that?"

"Yes, sir."

"I should like to know if anyone attempts to enter, especially
your uncle. Do you understand?"

"Yes, sir." But then finally lifting her eyes again: "You're not
afraid of him, are you? The murderer, I mean. You're not
afraid?"

"No."

"I didn't think so."

Thereafter the morning grew unsettling with a stagnant heat
that promised more rain, and brooding crowds waiting for provi-
sions along the docks. Now and again some passing citizen would

meet his gaze but generally they continued to keep their distance. Even later in a tavern filled with seasoned veterans of Bennington and Brandywine, it seemed that the consensus was still the same: there were aspects of this Revolution that were probably best left buried.

chapter
five

Tom Paine was a slender man with a large head and rather narrow shoulders. The nose, politely described as aquiline, had lately become the delight of cartoonists. The eyes, too, were said to have been somewhat birdlike . . . hence the popular conception of the man as a brooding eagle.

He was forty-three by this summer of the White Swan affair. His reputation, largely established with the publication of *Common Sense,* had recently suffered as the result of a dubious stance on the question of monies owed France. His fame, likewise established by earlier letters, had further begun to wane. (He was also broke, and only meagerly employed with the Pennsylvania

Assembly.) Yet for all these personal misfortunes he was still believed to possess a formidable mind and a certain quiet authority among congressional circles. He was also considered an honorable fellow, even if occasionally given to intrigue.

It was a Friday when Paine became associated with the White Swan affair. At this time the celebrated propagandist was still residing at the Indian Queen, and consequently a number of citizens were on hand to see Matty Grove appear. He came in the evening at an hour not usually reserved for visitors. A letter bearing Washington's signature served as an introduction. Actually Grove and Paine were acquainted, if not precisely friends. Shortly after Grove's credentials were delivered to Paine's room the propagandist appeared on the landing for a moment to greet Grove, then the doors were shut.

The room was low-beamed and narrow. Although apparently whitewashed not long before, the damp had once more left irregular stains across the plaster. Worms had attacked the wainscot and the arms of two chairs beside the grate. On entering, Grove found that his host had laid a decanter and two beaten cups on the table. There was no invitation to drink, however, and Paine remained seated on a cluttered divan.

"So. You have become the talk of the town," he said. "My condolences."

"If you prefer to meet later at some other place . . ."

Paine merely smiled. "Don't humor me, Matty Grove. My reputation has already been damaged if not destroyed. Now, if you wish to interrogate me, do so. But don't come around playing cat and mouse."

An actual cat lay sleeping on the cupboard between untidy stacks of folios. Another, an orange tabby, appeared to be watching from the hearth. There were nonetheless still signs of mice: gnawed edges of discarded books, pellets on the floorboards, even a tiny carcass.

"Very well, then it's a simple enough matter," Grove said. "As secretary to the Secret Committee you were responsible for the dissemination of confidential papers. I would like to know the procedure connected with that dissemination."

Although no longer smiling, Paine was still amused. "Tell me something. Do you always start at the bottom of the ladder and work up? Or am I to be the first for other reasons?"

"By rights, all such materials were to have been distributed according to need. I want to know if those rights were observed."

"And if I tell you that they were not, what then? The rack? The scourge? The brand?" He got up from the divan and moved to the table, where that decanter still lay untouched. "Look here, Grove, I've been apprised of your business in this city. Indeed, I've been apprised of it for some time. That doesn't mean, however, that I know anything more than the next man."

"And how much does the next man know of my business?"

"Only enough to stay clear of it." Having emptied the first cup, Paine now poured another—an inferior claret purchased from the tavern below. "Let's be frank, I'm aware that there is a list . . . a list of, say, two-score names? Two-score prestigious names? I am further aware that one of these prestigious gentlemen is believed to be a traitor, a profoundly formidable traitor responsible for a ghastly murder. Now, whether or not my name appears on that list is neither my business nor your concern. I will, however, say this: you do not know what you're getting into."

"And that is the opinion of Congress?"

"Not opinion. Truth. You may think the ground beneath your feet is firm, but it's not. It's ice, dangerously thin and deceptive ice."

Among sheaves of manuscripts and poorly bound volumes from a library lay what may have been the beginnings of another publication—a pamphlet, presumably intended to bolster a sagging morale. There may have also been more personal letters, but Grove could not make out the names of the addresses.

"Maybe I should pose the question differently," he said. "Maybe I should ask about a specific indiscretion."

"Smith and Dearborn were never names to me, Mr. Grove. Nor were they names to anyone in Congress."

"But their existence was known, their function."

"Vaguely known. Hardly more than a speculative rumor."

"Still, their reports must have been tangible enough. So one must have assumed that Washington had at least one spy within the British command."

"As a matter of fact there were those who maintained that Washington had actually fabricated the whole business to justify certain unpopular strategies."

"But more generally the reports were believed, were they not?"

"Insofar as we had no other measure of British intentions, yes."

"So when it was proposed that a traitor—"

"It was never proposed that plainly, Mr. Grove. At best there were only suggestions, and these were not taken altogether seriously."

"Well, someone took them seriously, Mr. Paine. I can assure you of that."

Grove drifted from the table to the mantle. Bills had been stuffed into a tin cup, an impressive roll of Continental currency rendered virtually worthless by inflation. There were also coins in a porcelain dish: a Spanish doubloon, a Bavarian carolin, even a few English coppers.

"Has it ever occurred to you, Mr. Grove, that our cause might be better served if you confined yourself to apprehending the murderer?"

"And leaving his master for another day?"

"For a better day. After all, imagine the glory of returning from some savage place with the White Swan killer in a cage."

Grove guessed there were promissory notes beneath a candlestick, also probably worthless.

"They say that one could never hope to keep the White Swan killer in a cage, Mr. Paine. That is, they say that the man is a ghost—an unusually elusive ghost."

Paine's smile again. "Then send him back to the land of the dead. Either way the cause will be served."

"And those lovers avenged?"

"Precisely."

Above the mantle hung a fanciful print of a pitched encounter between Pennsylvania riflemen and the King's Highlanders. Although clearly determined, the British were shown to be no match for this handful of rebels. Fanciful, thought Grove.

"Tell me something," Grove said at last. "Are you aware of the manner in which Smith and Dearborn were murdered?"

A hesitant shrug. "I was given to understand that a knife was employed."

"Not a knife. Some oddly fashioned blade, perhaps, but definitely not a knife. There was also a fair degree of mutilation that was not inflicted until after death."

"So?"

"So this is not a common murder, and therefore I'm not interested in common advice."

A second print, even more imaginative than the first, depicted Colonel Nixon reading the Declaration of Independence. Rather than the actual handful of sullen onlookers, the artist had filled his State House Yard with a jubilant throng of respectable citizens.

"Very well," Paine said suddenly, "let me put it another way. Although we all wish to see this matter resolved there are those who fear it might be resolved too roughly."

"And who would those be?"

"Various gentlemen in correspondence with me."

"John Adams?"

"If you must know, yes."

"Hancock?"

"Perhaps."

"Jefferson?"

Paine shook his head, retreating to the claret again. "Look, Mr. Grove, I have told you all that I know. Two spies were killed for reasons not yet determined. Beyond that I can only say that this is not a simple affair."

"Treason rarely is, Mr. Paine."

"Which is precisely my point. What might appear to be treason now may in fact be something else entirely . . . not ethical, perhaps, but necessary just the same."

"Meaning what?"

"Meaning that this war cannot be won with spit and breath. There is a need for both money and arms, and occasionally that need can be fulfilled only through compromise."

"And is that what happened to Smith and Dearborn? They were compromised?"

Paine pressed a thumb and finger to the bridge of his nose. "The nation is still a feeble infant, Mr. Grove. It may well die unless handled gently."

"The nation has not yet been born, Mr. Paine, and might still emerge as a monster. Now tell me what happened at the White Swan Inn."

"I'm sorry, but I can't help you. Now good night."

The night soon became unappealing again, with an infestation of mosquitoes and rumors of smallpox victims found aboard a drifting barge. Meanwhile at the Dwarf, it seemed that the child had once more been punished for some petty or imagined crime. Yet since the facts were still uncertain, Grove felt reluctant to intercede—and risk possibly compromising his mission.

chapter

six

It was early the next morning when Matty Grove was again seen in the streets of Philadelphia. The sultry wind from the night before had died. The rainclouds remained at a distance. Those who might have watched him pass along the broad street or adjoining lanes would have described his mood as pensive, possibly even meditative. He rode with a slack rein. His eyes were mainly fixed on the cobbles. On reaching the outskirts of the city he was observed turning west into the Highlands. Thereafter his business and destination became a matter of speculation.

The Highlands were still beautiful at this time with broad meadows of buttercups, and groves of hemlocks featured in local legends. Although no village proper had yet emerged, there were dozens of scattered cottages about. Some were elaborate, constructed in the old style and set on hills, others crude. Residents were solitary folk, descended from Scots and Welsh Quakers. Yet given the remoteness of these hills the place had also become a haven for outlaws, debtors and runaway slaves. These hills had also become the refuge of a certain John Clock, errant courier to the late Smith and Dearborn link.

It was late in the day when Grove approached Clock's cottage, following a crude map that Tallmadge had drawn on the back of a tavern bill. The light, although fading to the east, was more than sufficient along the rim of the hills. The cottage stood in black relief against the pines. From a distance there were only minimal signs of life: an axe embedded in a stump, a feeble vegetable plot. Then by degrees in the half-open door—Clock as a motionless sentinel.

He was a barrel of a man with a face as though cut from a rock. It was said Washington had originally recruited him to ferry dispatches across the Long Island Sound. Thereafter he had served in a number of related capacities before fixing himself to the Smith–Dearborn chain. In spite of popular stories to the contrary, his aforementioned leg had actually been lost beneath a wheel. The peg, however, was something to behold, ornately tooled in black locust. He was also known to carry a staff with the head of a griffon cut from walnut; yet emerging from the doorway of the cottage, it was a musket that he held in his arms.

"Go away, Matty Grove."

"I've brought a letter from Tallmadge."

"Go away before I cut you down."

"I've also brought you something to drink—assuming you're still in need of it."

There was no formal invitation to enter, merely a shrug and the door left ajar. Inside, the room was dark, barely head high. A straw pallet served as the bed, a trunk made do for a table. The remnants of a meal—black peas, a mess of clams and firecakes—

lay congealing in tin dishes. A coffeepot and shaving kit hung from nails on the wall.

"I should have killed you out there," Clock said. "I should have shot you where you stood."

"I've brought a letter, John."

"To hell with your letters. I should have shot you in the gut."

Originally Clock had been a peddler, and at least a corner of the room was devoted to his stock: pots and pans, rolls of shoddy lace, a crate of nails and plugs of tobacco.

"I've only come to ask a few questions," Grove said, "about what happened at the White Swan."

"To hell with the White Swan."

"According to Tallmadge you were the courier to Fairfield."

"I was the fool."

"He also says that the dispatchers were collected from the common and then ferried over the Devil's Gate. The boatman went by the name of Brewster."

"Another damn fool."

"I'd like to know the details."

Rum was poured, the dregs of a local brew that Clock favored. Then retreating to the corner of the room, Clock slowly sagged to the pallet. Although his expression remained unchanged, his face was tracked with tears.

"I never knew them, least not in the normal way. But you get a feeling for people when you carry their secrets. You get a sense of them."

"How were you alerted that a dispatch was ready to be collected?"

Clock shuddered with another mouthful of rum. "Various signs on the Maiden Lane."

"What sort of signs?"

"Circle in chalk on the post, a pair of sticks at the crossroads."

"And the dispatches were then retrieved from the north end of the common?"

"From what they call the Shoemaker's Lot near Tanneries. I'd usually make the rounds at dusk—not so early as broad daylight, not so late as to draw suspicion. And the absence of this leg helped . . . who would imagine that bloody George Washington would hire a courier with a damn stump?"

"And after the job was done?"

"Back through the lines with more help from the leg. You see, that's where I'd keep the goods—rolled up in this here pegleg, 'specially hollowed out for the purpose."

"And they never searched?"

"Never so they found it."

Clock had his head inclined to the window. Grove guessed he had spent the better part of the last six weeks in just such a posture: eyes fixed on the distant hills, tin cup in hand, bottle at his knee.

"Tell me about the last night," Grove said.

"What about it?"

There were additional bottles by the pallet, also a cudgel and worn Bible—all testimony that the nights had been the worst of it.

"It was Friday," Grove said. "According to Ben Tallmadge's record you were still in New York."

"Damn the record."

"You boarded near William Street in a place called the Drum. You generally dined on the premises and only conducted a nominal business."

"I was sick, sick with the chill."

"Meanwhile, and unknown to you, Smith and Dearborn were about to leave. We can only guess at what actually prompted their flight, but we know that they were definitely on the road by Friday evening."

"They were also probably sick, sick with fear of it."

"But their progress was slow, mostly because of a critical detour to lay another packet in the field."

The eyes responded first. Clock's head was still inclined to the window but his eyes briefly shifted back to Grove. "I was a sick man, I hardly left my bed."

"The theory is that the packet must have been dropped just as they left the city," Grove went on. "Obviously a risky venture, but considered important enough to warrant it."

"I was sick, I tell you. I didn't even know the time of day."

"Nightfall. Not the best time to travel, but under the circumstances—"

"Look, I'm not your traitor, Grove. I'm just the courier."

"Yes, you are the courier, Mr. Clock. You are charged with the collection and delivery of packets. You are alerted by various signs on the Maiden Lane, then directed to the common. All in all a simple enough task, assuming one doesn't lose his nerve."

Again it was the eyes—a hesitant glance to Grove, a falling gaze to the floorboards. Finally very quietly: "You get a sense of the roads after a time, a sense of when it's safe and when it's not. And the worst of it's like a chill—a hard chill. First you feel it in the chest, then in the limbs. But it's not only inside you. It's everywhere, a sniff of death."

"So you fled the city."

A nod. "Aye."

"But not before passing the Maiden Lane."

"Aye."

"And the signs were there?"

"A pair of sticks, like crossed bones."

"But you ignored them?"

"Aye."

For a while neither spoke, the wind suddenly clattering over the brow of the hill.

"Someone will have to return," Grove finally said. "That last packet probably cost them their lives. The least we can do is collect it."

"While also collecting a noose, or a butcher's knife."

"If you're still unwilling I can send—"

"Didn't say I was unwilling. Just said I didn't much feel like dying for a mess of bloody papers."

"I can give you an escort from Fairfield."

"The devil with your escort. I'd sooner trust my own one leg to the two of yours."

"And there's payment."

"I'm not a coward, Grove. I may not want to end up in little pieces but I'm not a coward. If I ran that night it was only because of the moment . . . the chill. I'm not one to leave anyone's legacy rotting in the ground, least of all from my own flock."

It had grown dark by now, Clock becoming a hunched silhouette.

"It's not just that killer you're after, is it?" he said. "There's more to it than that, isn't there?"

"Possibly."

"And my lambs were murdered because they sensed it, eh?"

"Perhaps."

"Well, then you'd better keep your wits about you, because there's a beast out there the likes of which neither of us has seen before."

Matty Grove wondered which beast Clock meant—the killer, or his employer.

Although it was again late when Matty Grove returned to the Dwarf, a number of citizens were still on hand to observe him: Drapier, the loquacious Mr. Hatch, two or three irregular patrons who had lately taken an interest in this case. As usual, Grove had nothing to say to anyone . . . except, of course, the child.

She saw him first in the passage just as he had mounted the stairs. In the half-light of a weak candle he appeared ominous. Yet on closer inspection she sensed something she had not seen before —worry, maybe regret. It was not so much in the near-whispered voice as what seemed to lie behind it.

"Where was your uncle today?"

"Just about the house."

"But not in my quarters?"

"No, sir."

"Nor the others?"

"Not to my knowledge, sir."

Then leaning against the jamb, briefly shutting his eyes: "Good enough."

Thereafter she heard him pacing for at least an hour, and in the morning another empty bottle had been laid at the door.

chapter

seven

The first consignment of papers arrived on a Tuesday. At about ten o'clock in the morning three discreet clerks in plain suits appeared at the Dwarf asking to see Matty Grove. They carried two brass-bound trunks and a portmanteau suspended from the shoulder by a strap. "And what is your business with Mr. Grove?" the proprietor demanded.

Of course he did not receive an answer.

Moments after Grove had ushered the young men into his chamber they reappeared without their luggage. Grove was then not seen for some six hours, although his footsteps were heard, back and forth from wall to wall.

Naturally there was speculation about what sort of papers were inside those brass-bound trunks and that shabby portmanteau. There were those, led by Drapier, who held that the papers were personal letters Grove had requested to blackmail the authors.

On the other side of this speculative wall Mr. Jameson Hatch maintained that the papers consisted of congressional records Grove had acquired to understand better the soil, the background, of this story. This was not the whole truth but it was close.

The papers were, in fact, of three categories. There were the minutes and memoranda from various military committees. There were letters and observations on the progress of the war as a whole and there were biographical notes on certain revolutionary figures.

Grove's possession of these papers caused no small degree of alarm. "By rights, I shouldn't even let you touch them," Tallmadge said when he and Grove met that evening in a groggery near the wharf. "Indeed, by rights we shouldn't even be having this talk."

It was a place filled with sailors from foreign vessels and the less respectable jobbers. Tallmadge had managed to secure a private booth, but only after slipping the proprietor a shilling.

"There's also the question of expediency," Tallmadge said. "I mean, not all of this material can be of value."

"The value is set by an inspection of the goals, Benjamin."

"Yes, but at what cost? I don't suppose I need tell you that complaints have been lodged—serious complaints."

"From whom?"

"It doesn't matter."

"Tom Paine?" Grove asked, noting the petrified head of an Iroquois warrier encased in a bell jar above the bar.

"Let me put it another way," Tallmadge said. "Although I shouldn't wish you to leave any stone unturned, I really see no reason why you can't use a little discretion. Besides, there's still the matter of your own reputation to consider."

"What's that supposed to mean?"

"It *means* that there are those who may argue that your motives are too personal, that you have always resented those privileged by birth and are using this affair as an excuse to persecute them." A quick glance to meet Grove's eyes. "Well, it's true, isn't it? You've never trusted those with money, have you?"

A barmaid passed. He waited. "My personal feelings have nothing to do with this, Benjamin. You tell me a traitor has sprung from some rarified, privileged ground. Well, then I think we should at least get some understanding of that ground."

Tallmadge shook his head, as though not hearing. "And there's also John Clock, not the most reliable fellow. Did I mention he almost undid us at Fairfield?"

"The situation is different and he knows it."

"The situation is critical and it would seem that I'm the only one who knows it." . . .

The nights were most productive, partly because of the quiet and partly because of Grove's nature. He consumed his meals, such as they were, at odd intervals. He would often leave a plate untouched for hours, then pick at it like a rat. The drink was consumed somewhat more regularly but never before dusk. Now and again, usually after midnight, he walked the streets. Otherwise the pages held his attention until dawn.

As for his method, it would be safe to say that what he had told Tallmadge was essentially true—this was a time for testing the ground. By the same token, however, this was further a time for assemblage, which was often an intuitive process. Beginning with the fundamental assumption that his quarry was a man of means, he spent the first six or seven hours trying to locate corroborative evidence with the broader record. He turned to letters from abroad—letters from stock-jobbers in Madrid and Martinique, reports from agents in London and the Netherlands. He also found himself drawn to the dispatches from certain merchants in Paris, ostensibly charged with procuring arms for this Revolution but in fact procuring nothing but a profit.

Although there were moments when his progress seemed haphazard, by the end of the fourth night he could point to his notes and tell Tallmadge that Smith and Dearborn had been correct— this was no ordinary traitor. "Indeed, he's definitely a man of wide affiliations."

Yes, but what *sort* of affiliations? Tallmadge said.

"International," Grove responded, while pointing to three key documents.

The first was a report from an agent in Boston who claimed that the British possessed too much knowledge of American dealings abroad to be passed off as coincidence. Next were the confessions of a Hessian deserter who claimed that his English commander seemed to know the tonnage and cargo of nearly every foreign vessel unloading on American soil. Finally there was Miss Dearborn's original assertion that the British would have never taken such enormous pains to preserve the identity of an *ordinary* spy.

He tended to work slowly through these nights, reminding himself that a man tended to see what he wanted to see, and that by definition a traitor was an amorphous creature. Although he liked to believe that his progress was a deductive path from firm truth to the less firm, he was equally aware that what Tallmadge had said was also true—that Matty Grove had never trusted those with wealth and power, not after an impoverished childhood and four bitter years in the ragtag rebel army.

And there were moments when he felt driven by the thrill of the hunt, but for the most part this was fairly tedious work. He tended to remain seated for about an hour at a time, then would suddenly rise without thinking and continue to pace again. Although there was much wasted effort, he told himself that this story was a hunt, and so one had to expect the road to wind back on itself.

He also spent some time worrying about that one-legged courier, Mr. Clock, en route from New York, but consoled himself with the thought that in spite of appearances, this White Swan monster was, after all, just another man.

Was he not?

chapter
eight

The house was old, almost reminiscent of an earlier era, with low eaves and a coffin door. The rear roof, descending from ridge to wing, was also something rarely seen in those days. There were traces of fire here and there, scorched brick and timber. Otherwise the primary cause of ruin had simply been neglect. A dying oak stood in the yard. The garden had been reduced to nothing.

Presumably the house had been one of several dwellings allotted as a way station. Some had formerly belonged to sympathizers of the Crown. A few had just been abandoned. Most were under the care and formal ownership of trusted intermediaries, often widows or prematurely retired officers. During the dark months of the British occupation these dwellings had been highly guarded secrets. By this summer of 1780, however, they were largely a convenience for errant spies and couriers like Mr. John Clock.

It was a Friday when Clock reached this place, approaching by a devious route from a lesser road south of the highway. His hostess was a shrewd little woman by the name of Fanny Blair. Mrs. Blair was an old hand at this game, having received numerous frightened couriers since her house had been established. Yet never had there been someone quite as terrified as Mr. Clock.

They dined on fish pies, an oyster stew, rice and beer. It was a bleak night. Clock said very little at first, only that he had just come from New York and what a damn place it was with Redcoats on every corner and Tories that would make you sick.

"And what were you doing in New York?" Mrs. Blair asked, not expecting an answer.

"What do you think I was doing?" he snapped, then proceeded to relate a garbled story about how he had just retrieved a secret packet from a place that they called the Shoemaker's Lot.

She pushed her plate aside. "Do you know what I think, Mr. Clock? I think I'll pretend that I didn't hear that. Aye, I didn't hear a word you said."

He gave her a sideways glance, drumming his fingers on the table. "There's no harm in knowing what I done. The harm's in not being prepared for what might come after."

She shook her head. "You're drunk, John Clock. You're drunk as a newt."

" 'Course, I'm drunk. But that doesn't mean you shouldn't be prepared—"

"Prepared for what?"

He leaned forward, gripping the edges of the table. "I think he may have followed me here, followed me all the way down from New York City."

"Who are you talking about? *Who* followed you?"

"He doesn't have a name. He's a werewolf."

She shook her head again with an indulgent smile. "Like I said, Mr. Clock, you're drunk as a newt."

It must have been about midnight when the killer entered, probably circling once or twice, before employing a bit of string and a stick to unlatch the scullery door. Years ago Mrs. Blair had kept a dog to guard against intruders but now there was only a cat.

From the scullery he moved to the parlor, but very lightly because the floorboards there were loose. So he kept along the edges of things, and crept on the balls of his feet.

He did leave a trace of mud at the bottom of the staircase, another on the landing, but all in all he didn't so much as disturb the dust on the panes. It wasn't until he had reached the passage that Mrs. Blair was even aware of the possibility of an intruder. And then it was hardly more than a breeze beneath the door, or a settling timber.

Now, of course, she knew there were no such things as *were-wolves,* but all the same she couldn't help but imagine some weird transformation as the possible intruder passed along the corridor . . . the hair advancing in a thick mane from the neck, the jawbone stretching to form a snout, the fangs extending past the lower lip.

Damn Mr. Clock and his drunken talk.

She lay very still, eyes shut tight, right hand clenched around a candlestick. Although there were two stout walls separating Clock's room from her own, she heard the sounds . . .

Mr. Clock was fast asleep and dreaming after one glass too many. Finally waking up as the door swung open, he at first mistook the intruder for Mrs. Blair's nephew, who fancied himself a poet and occasionally spent nights en route from New Jersey.

But her nephew was a frail lad, a timid soul, and certainly not one to enter a man's chamber in the dead of night with a knife poorly concealed beneath his coat.

65

The Traitor

And what a knife—broad and firm, and sharp as a razor.

No tries of terror came from him, not at first. Only a series of muffled grunts and the clatter of a chamber pot. Then sounds of shattering glass, a ripping sheet and that pegleg thumping on the floorboards. Followed by a long scream, and silence.

A minute passed, maybe two. Mrs. Blair saw in her mind's eye the creature resting—seated on his haunches, gazing at his victim's body with enormous yellow eyes. The tongue would be drooping past the jowls as the ears fell and the mangy head cocked to the side. At last she heard him moving again, drawing back the curtains for light, bolting the door.

She couldn't help but seeing it all in her mind's eye—and actually hearing the cutting and the slashing.

"Apparently they're sending a physician," Tallmadge was saying, "although I don't know who's to be the patient."

It was not late—barely ten in the morning, or less than three hours since the word had begun to spread. Approximately twenty members of the local militia had gathered in the forecourt while smaller parties had begun a search for the highroad. Although no one apart from Tallmadge had yet entered the room, some sense of what lay inside must have been established in everyone's mind. On the arrival of Matty Grove it was all confirmed.

"I take it no one heard or saw anything?" Grove asked.

Tallmadge shook his head. "Nothing that can be counted on. The local word is that the murderer was a turnskin—"

"Turnskin?"

"It's from the Latin *Versipellis*. It means werewolf. Don't laugh. The woman, Mrs. Blair, recalls noting an unearthly stench." Then catching a look in Grove's eyes, "Well, if you actually saw the body I think you'd understand, not that I'm suggesting you go up there. I wouldn't recommend anyone going up there. I've a theory," Tallmadge said, "if you want to hear it."

Grove shrugged, hand tapping against his thigh. "I should never have sent him out in the first place—"

"It was a calculated risk that had to be taken. And if nothing else it proves you were right—there was definitely a last packet."

"Then where is it?"

"Well, that's the whole point, isn't it? Clock was murdered so that it could be retrieved."

"You searched the room?"

"And the wagon."

"What about . . . his leg?"

"I told you, Matty, it's the same as the last time. The body has been altogether—"

"I mean the pegleg. Did you examine it?"

Tallmadge turned to the house, hands slipping from his side. "Bloody hell. I'm a damned fool, aren't I?"

There were several dominant odors inside: wet ash, burned tallow, rotting timber. On leaving Tallmadge below and ascending the staircase, Grove also caught the vaguely sweet smell of dung. At first look, however, nothing seemed amiss. Merely plates and cutlery had not been cleared from the table, bread crumbs had attracted mice. But along the last passage to the bedroom—a handprint in blood, and traces of an undigested meal.

Although the bedroom door had been left ajar nothing was immediately clear. A strip of light from a shattered window revealed only a small amount of blood and clothing flung to the floor. Then by degrees, as his eyes grew accustomed to the darkness: more blood on the walls, a larger pool beside the bed.

He hesitated in the doorway a long time before entering the room: a discarded boot, a chamber pot, fragments of soil and glass where the murderer had obviously entered. Then by degrees: a pale arm and shoulder amid the tangled sheets.

He waited several moments before approaching the bed. Footprints, distinct in blood, marked where the killer had stood. A second handprint, also distinct, suggested a momentary pause. There were further signs of a struggle: an arc of blood across the ceiling as if splattered by a flailing arm, another desperate print extending to a candlestick. Finally there was some indication that Clock had ended up on his knees in a corner, as if attempting to burrow through the plaster.

In all probability Clock had died twice—first on receiving a cut to the throat, then the mutilation. The face, however, bore no signs of it. The eyes were peacefully shut. The head lay almost naturally on the shoulder. Only the left hand, partially severed at the wrist, still seemed taut with rage. Beyond the bed were traces of blood in unusual places: the water basin, a looking glass, a chair where the murderer may have briefly caught his breath. The rest was much as expected: intestines removed and laid to the shoulder, appendages severed and tossed to the floor, a quantity of sand and limestone deposited in the mouth. From the bed there were tracks to the ends of the room where the killer had clearly conducted a search of Clock's personal effects: clothing, traveling kit, anything large enough to accommodate a few inches of paper. The ornately tooled pegleg, however, had evidently not been touched.

It took the better part of fifteen minutes to detach the wooden limb. As Grove worked he kept his eyes fixed on the wall, and a single mosquito drawn by the blood. When he had the thing in his hands he moved back out into the corridor and shut the door. The pegleg was lighter than expected, owing to that secret cavity especially hollowed out for the purpose.

He shut his eyes against a wave of nausea as his hand slipped into the recess, opened them as his fingers encountered the oilskin. It was handstitched and rolled to the diameter of a musket barrel but contained at least a dozen pages. Some appeared to be on rather plain stock, but others were clearly with His Majesty's seal.

*   *   *

There were sixteen pages, all from the same hand. What may have been a salutation appeared boldly across the top of the first. Thereafter each line was mainly composed of numerals. The numerals had been arranged in groups of three and four digits, broken only by the occasional word. The words, mostly articles and proper names, were hardly more enlightening.

To examine these pages Tallmadge and Grove went to a carriage at the edge of the forecourt. Called a landau, it was a fairly elegant thing that had formerly belonged to a British major with profits from this war. Although the upholstery had worn poorly the fittings were still intact: a regimental crest impressed on the door, a lantern for night travel. For the moment, however, the twilight was enough.

"I don't suppose we have any way of determining whether these are genuine," Tallmadge said.

"I'm sure they are."

"But not from the woman's hand, nor Smith's."

"They were stolen, Benjamin, apparently a last desperate act."

Tallmadge had turned to the fifth page. A certain amount of Clock's blood had seeped through the oilskin, leaving a stain that vaguely resembled a dog. There were further traces of Clock's blood on the oilskin. "Very well, but even assuming you're right, why would they have taken the risk?"

"Because they believed the game was up, and also because they believed in it."

"So they lifted the king's packet?"

"Or rifled Henry Clinton's office . . . because as British commander-in-chief he would obviously have a direct line to London."

Tallmadge lifted another page, the seventh—more blood in the shape of a star.

Grove said, "Look, I'm not sure, but we've seen this kind of cipher before, haven't we? Substitutional, certain numerals would represent line and page of a book . . . a dictionary, maybe. Others would represent an alphabetic substitution . . . which only requires the identification of a key."

Still another page mottled with Clock's blood. "One could spend weeks on this sort of thing and still gain nothing," Tallmadge said.

"Then again one could make no attempt at all and *definitely* gain nothing."

They left the carriage and began to walk, once more drawing glances from the ranks—some suspicious, some bored. Although no Pennsylvania regiment had yet formally mutinied, rumors had been circulating since the spring.

"Why do you suppose it happened here?" Tallmadge said at last.

Even the constabulary had paused to watch.

"Why not?"

"Well, I should think it would have been a matter of convenience if nothing else. I mean, assuming Clock had been marked the moment he collected the packet, why wasn't he taken sooner? There must have been opportunity on the road?"

Grove shrugged. "I imagine it was felt that the message they left would be more pronounced here—on our own ground."

"The message?"

"That in the end none of us is safe."

An aftermath to the murder of John Clock was an outcry from several quarters for a swift and decisive revenge. There was also a letter, another *public* letter drafted in part by Tom Paine. Although ostensibly a call to arms against an outrageous British menace, the letter contained a secondary message between the lines—a cutting note for Matty Grove and all those who supported him. In essence it was that this White Swan affair had by now become a personal duel of wits between two unmatched adversaries. Of course there was no direct pronouncement that

Grove was bound to lose, but the suggestion was clear enough.

Whether in response or not, for two days following Grove hardly left his room. There, admitting no one but young Sarah, he spent his time brooding over the unintelligible notes that still bore traces of the courier's blood. A running tally of his drinking habits revealed two bottles of madeira consumed on the first day, at least as many on the second.

chapter
nine

The cryptographer himself was known, if only as a local eccentric and student of unusual phenomena. His name was Monk—Arthur James Monk. His residence consisted of two cluttered rooms above an apothecary's shop. His claim to fame—such as it was—rested largely on his brief study with Benjamin Franklin, and he regularly corresponded with Mr. Jefferson in Virginia. He was also said to possess an extensive collection of strange artifacts from beyond the Ohio, including the bone fragments of a mammoth and the fangs of an uncommonly large cat.

Physically he was a small man with reddish hair and a pale complexion. His age was somewhere between thirty and forty. He walked with a slight limp since an accident as a child and was otherwise not an agile man. The features were, some said, vaguely Semitic, not surprising considering a vein of Jewish blood. His eyes were blue; vision slightly myopic from hours spent poring over maps of the western lands, which were also said to be his passion.

It was a Wednesday when the gnomic Mr. Monk became a participant in the White Swan inquiry. Talk of the courier's death was still rife, while the dour Matty Grove had seemingly grown more remote than ever. Because of the weather and hour of the day—a fog-bound evening—it was doubtful that anyone actually saw Grove arrive. He was directed to the door by a boy employed below, and was received in what passed for a sitting room.

The room, poorly lit and irregularly shaped, seemed less suited for living than for storage. Apart from a low sofa and armchair, the furnishings were like something from a medical college: drawing boards heaped with unbound notes, shelves resting on blocks of wood, a warped commode and carpenter's bench littered with optical instruments.

It began on a cool note, a mumbled introduction and passing reference to Tallmadge. Then, although Grove had not yet withdrawn the pages in question, the purpose of his visit must have been evident. Monk had even produced a reading lamp, a contraption of his own invention designed for detailed work.

"I suppose I should confess that strictly speaking this is not my province," he told Grove. "Puzzles, yes. Not mysteries."

"Is there such a difference?"

"Definitely. The puzzle is for enjoyment, the mystery apparently involves life and death." He took out a neatly clipped column of newsprint from between the pages of an almanac—one more grisly account of the courier's story. "The fact is, I happen to know that at least one person has already died over this matter —not to mention the original two."

"People are dying every day in this war, Mr. Monk."

"Not the way they died at the White Swan. Besides, I'm not really all that accomplished at this sort of thing—"

"Tallmadge seems to think you are."

"Tallmadge is too kind. I can take a look but make no promises beyond that."

A table was cleared, a sagging card table previously covered with odd diagrams, the remains of a meal and more yellowed bone fragments. The lantern was lit and set so that the light fell at an optimum angle. Grove then laid down the packet—those sixteen pages still faintly tracked with Clock's blood.

Monk's first pronouncements were elementary. The basic form, he said, was common enough, in that the numerals referred a reader to one of two substitutional codes. The first, comprising approximately a third of the text, employed a code book of some obviously standard text. The second, comprising the majority of the text, employed an alphabetic cipher. The message was the product of an educated hand but was undoubtedly written at one sitting—hence the gradual deterioration of penmanship.

"How long would it have taken someone to produce such a thing?" Grove asked.

"That would depend on one's familiarity with the keys. The whole point of employing two ciphers is to facilitate speed."

"Approximately, then."

Another glance at the pages to determine their weight. "Approximately four hours."

"And to decipher them at the other end?"

"Two, perhaps less."

"And with what degree of sophistication?"

"Little or none. The system is based on trust—trust between the parties. A child could make sense of this, assuming he had the keys."

"And without them?"

"That remains to be seen. It would, however, help if you were to enlighten me as to their source."

Grove moved to the window, and a view of the fog-bound lane below. An equally obscure map of the western plains had been tacked to the wall above. "Such as?"

"Who was the author?"

"We're not sure."

"But certainly neither of those two murdered spies, correct?"

"Yes."

"And where exactly was the letter to have been sent?"

"I can only guess."

"London?"

"Probably."

"His Majesty's throne?"

"Perhaps."

"But beyond that you have no notion of what the thing might be about?" Then catching a glimpse of Grove's eyes: "Well, surely there's no harm in asking."

They were both standing now . . . Grove still inspecting that dubious map of the West, Monk poised a few paces behind him. A second map, likely no more reliable than the first, purported to trace the Missouri River as far as the Pacific.

"I don't imagine that you ever think about it much, do you?" Monk said softly. "I mean, in the purely geographical sense."

"Think about what?"

A third map, presumably from Monk's own plump and tiny hand, was virtually unrecognizable.

"The continent, the sheet size of it. Do you realize, for example, that the whole of Europe could quite easily fit into that ocean of grass out there?"

"I don't think Europe gives a damn, Mr. Monk."

"Ah, but it does. It must. I mean, ultimately what else is at stake apart from the physical control of the land? Nothing." He withdrew still another map to reveal the fractured skull of an aborigine. Then after a moment's silence: "They say that you're actually hunting two men, Mr. Grove—not only the White

75

Swan killer, but the traitor who employed him as well. Is that true?"

Apparently a bit of rock still lay embedded in the cranium. "More or less."

"They also say that although you are a formidable hunter you may have met your match. Also true?"

Grove said nothing.

"Not that I mean to pry, but it's helpful to know where one stands."

Grove received the coroner's report on John Clock at ten o'clock that same evening. The author was the celebrated Dr. Benjamin Rush. Based on an examination of the wounds, it was determined that the weapon had been some sort of a broad-handled hatchet of primitive design. The triangular blade was not dissimilar in shape to those found among various African tribes. The method of butchery also suggested a barbarous African rite. Attached to these pages were several supplementary diagrams and notes that Grove did not bother to read. Indeed, before the night was through he laid the whole of it in the fire.

chapter
ten

At four o'clock the following afternoon Grove and Tallmadge met in an outlying tavern called the Black League. It was an infrequently patronized place, largely catering to strangers and employees of a failing mill. The proprietor was a reticent woman, not much given to gossip. Nor were the servants likely to betray anything of what was seen or heard. Even the weather was seemingly conducive to secrecy, with intermittent rain and a woodland fog.

They drank ale, something real and reliable. Tallmadge smoked, ignoring a bowl of clams he had ordered before Grove's arrival. The proprietor had gone off, leaving a girl to tend the tables. A portrait of the king had been crudely transformed into the likeness of Washington. Between them on the table lay ten or twelve pages of Grove's personal notes—the fruit of previous nights' work. Although many pages were all but illegible, the thrust seemed clear enough with the names of another dozen gentlemen possibly guilty of treason.

The names had been listed on a single sheet of yellow rag torn from a penny notebook. Tallmadge had read them twice, once at a glance, then again with more care. When he finally spoke his voice sounded remote. "May I ask why you included young Mr. Hamilton?"

Grove shrugged. "Why not? You included him on your list."

"Did I? Well, I must have been desperate."

"He also has the means, financially speaking."

"But no motive."

"No apparent motive."

"And His Excellency trusts him."

"All the more reason why we shouldn't. The time has come, Benjamin, to focus on people with the *capacity* for treason, not just the inclination."

"Then why include congressmen who are no longer even serving?"

"Because even a waning influence shouldn't be discounted."

"All right, but what about the rest? Robert Morris, for example. Why include him?"

"I think the size of his purse is reason enough for suspicion."

"The man is a *merchant,* Matty. It's his business to improve money—"

"Exactly."

"And on the whole he's taken big risks on behalf of this movement."

"But rarely if ever without a profit." A pause, toying with a plug of tobacco: "Listen to me, Benjamin, I'm not suggesting that these men are the only ones under suspicion. On the contrary, the list is arbitrary. There are others who could easily replace them or be added. But the common denominator to them all is something we can't ignore—money."

"The proverbial root of all evil?"

"Call it what you like, but the man we are looking for is, definitely, someone with funds—substantial funds."

"Did you know that Robert Morris has virtually raised three regiments with funds from his own pocket?"

"Which in turn would give him control of those regiments . . . Benjamin, I'm convinced our traitor is a merchant."

A dray appeared in the yard below. Laden with West Indian rum, every drop might well have also represented someone's undue profit.

"I suppose I should warn you that these gentlemen represent a rather formidable pack," Tallmadge finally said.

"Owing to the contents of their pockets?"

"If you like."

"Nonetheless they must be examined. After all, we aren't looking for some devious clerk or messenger. We're looking for a man of *means*—means to acquire secrets, to direct others, to employ a uniquely qualified butcher when required."

Another pause while Tallmadge glanced again at that yellow scrap of paper. "I repeat, these are powerful figures, Matty."

"Yes, but who are they lending their power to? And to what end?"

"Even a casual inquiry might lead to scandal."

"We already have a bloody scandal."

"Very well, let me put it another way. Although I don't mean to curtail your movements I'd like you at least to watch your step —so as not to tread on important toes—"

"And thereby cause important voices to cry out in pain?"

"Washington isn't invulnerable, Matty."

"Washington can't have it both ways. If you want me to solve these White Swan murders I must be free to follow whatever clues present themselves."

"Meaning what?"

"Meaning that I must have room to maneuver, to investigate, to question whomever I wish."

"And you wish to question the men on this list?"

"Possibly. Eventually . . ."

"Then at least do it *carefully* . . . these aren't exactly men to be trifled with."

"I thought no man was to be trifled with, Benjamin. Come to think of it, I thought that was the whole point of this so-called Revolution."

They parted at the edge of a chestnut grove and a disused patch of land adjacent to the mill. Some years back there had been a pitched encounter here, a brief but bloody affair between His Majesty's Forty-second Foot and members of a local brigade. Following an initial success with bayonet, the British left themselves hopelessly exposed to fire from the rise. Now even the more skeptical inhabitants claimed to have heard the Scots pipes on otherwise silent nights . . .

"By the way," Tallmadge said abruptly, "I failed to ask what resulted from your meeting with my Mr. Monk. Has he agreed to help?"

Grove was stripping leaves off a vine he had picked without thinking. "Within limits."

"But he fears the political ramifications, I suppose."

"He fears a knife in the belly, Benjamin."

Among the deeper bracken one might have even found physical reminders of that skirmish: shattered canteens, gilded brass buttons, shoulder plates and powder horns. Several trees further bore scars from volleys returned from the glade . . .

"There's a possibility that I may soon have something of interest regarding our monster," Tallmadge added. "Nothing definite but it seems that last year a certain rifleman was said to have butchered a British foraging party, in an altogether too familiar manner."

"Meaning what?"

"That a number of the bodies had been dismembered."

"Locally?"

"In the west."

"Have you a name?"

"Not yet."

"A physical description?"

"At this point it's only a rumor, Matty, a tale told around campfires."

"But not one to be ignored."

"Of course not. It's merely that . . ." He hesitated again peering through the foliage at what might have been a disintegrating cartridge box. "Well, you *will* observe some caution, won't you?"

"I shall only be talking to a pack of merchants, Benjamin."

"But talk does have a way of getting out of hand, particularly in *that* society." Another pause, gazing at leaves that might have been scattered bank notes. "I simply mean to say that you would do well to watch your back from this day forward."

"Are you implying that I may soon find myself in dishonorable company?" Grove smiled.

"I'm implying that this is a dangerous business, and one should take precautions."

Then as if to emphasize the point, Tallmadge produced a new acquisition from his saddlebag: an officer's carbine loaded with swan shot. Although an ungainly thing, it was particularly suited for close-quarter work in darkness.

The evening began with Grove's arrival at the Dwarf and the child obviously frightened while Drapier prowled the corridors with the meddlesome Mr. Hatch. There was a fog, a particularly noisome incursion with a stench of the marshland. In the streets, there was definitely someone's shadow thrown against the brickwork of an empty lane.

It was now quite late. Grove had left his room out of restlessness. Although his attention had been earlier drawn by the clap of a boot heel on cobbles, it was not until the High Street market that he actually sensed the presence of someone behind him.

The lanes were quite narrow here, hardly more than cartways between the stalls. Although lanterns had been suspended from the pillared brick, the dank enclosures were lit only from the alleys. There were also less obvious passages between the sheds that Grove had assumed would be to his advantage.

At first he moved to the alcove of a butchery, a foul place littered with meat scraps and cuttings. Although some light fell from the rafters, the recess was sufficiently dark. After a moment's hesitation he knelt to withdraw the knife sheathed in his boot . . . then after another moment withdrew the pistol instead. The load consisted of three buckshot behind a ball.

He waited until the footsteps were close before moving again. Then avoiding brittle cabbage leaves and shards of pottery, he slipped back into the lane. His left hand, formally at his side, now gradually lifted to brace his right. The pistol, too, rose by degrees. For a moment there was the suggestion of a target—a half-formed vision of something huge and misshapen. Then between a row of stalls—another glimpse of steel and buckskin. Yet each time he advanced, his quarry somehow vanished into the brickwork.

In all he spent almost an hour chasing this impossibly elusive shadow before finally giving up: clothing drenched with perspiration, hand no longer dead steady. The wind had risen with the stench of something he could not place.

On returning to the Dwarf he again found the child in tears, presumably after suffering another beating. Under the circumstances, however, he hardly felt able to comfort her.

chapter
eleven

The following morning signaled a warm and humid day. Popular attention had apparently turned to the east, where thirteen men from the First New York were said to have been shot for mutiny. There was also some excitement over the flogging of a whore in the Strawberry Alley.

It was just after ten o'clock when Matty Grove arrived unannounced at a modest trading house near the docks. There he was met by a red-haired young man in an elegant suit by the name of Robert La Salle. After an exchange of amenities—for the sake of the junior clerks—the two withdrew to a richly appointed inner chamber where conversation could not be overheard. An excellent coffee was offered, a delicate blend imported by roundabout means from Holland. There was also an equally impressive claret.

It began on a congenial note, a happy reminiscence from three years before when on Grove's suggestion this Mr. Robert La Salle had first established himself as a foreign merchant in order to spy on British concerns. Next, without revealing his motives, Grove posed one or two questions of a general nature regarding trade in Martinique. Then following a reference to the price of Caribbean powder, they moved to the crux of the matter: the secret trade that kept this war in progress.

Grove said he was interested in the larger trading houses, those with broad international ties. At the moment, however, he was not necessarily mentioning names.

"Nevertheless, am I to understand that we are discussing houses with conflicting interests?" La Salle said. "Houses with, say, fingers in several pots?"

"It's hardly more than conjecture at this point, Robert. I'm only wondering who in the community is capable of . . . of treason."

"Oh, but they're all *capable* of treason, Matty. Now if you were to ask me who's capable of arranging those White Swan murders . . . well, that's a different question."

"And the answer?"

A smile. "Actually, I'm not certain."

A ledger was produced, a rather impressively bound quarto in goatskin. The escritoire from which it came was equally impressive with a marquetry of tortoise shell. At the moment, though, La Salle called Grove's attention to an etching on the wall, an extravagant vision of a Caribbean bay as if seen from aboard ship.

That, La Salle said, was the key to it all—the port at St. Eustatia. Although there were dozens of commercial houses with business in foreign harbors, to grasp the scope of their profits one had to understand the West Indian trade, particularly as conducted at St. Eustatia. Physically the island was nothing—a bit of rock six miles long and barely three in breadth. Yet given her geographical position—St. Kitts to the southeast, St. Bartholomew to the north, St. Croix and the Greater Antilles just beyond—nature ordained her as an international port. Which was to say, La Salle added, that regardless of the British blockade there was nothing that could not be purchased—not muskets, not powder, not even cannon.

"And where do these goods come from?" Grove asked.

"Various places."

"Holland? France?"

"By all means."

"England?"

"On occasion . . . but we are still discussing legitimate trade, Matty . . . or at least passably legitimate. Goods are shipped from manufacturer to recognized agents long before they reach Statia. It's only later that diversions are made."

"And apart from military stores, what else is available? Linens? Nails? Cordage?"

"At the very least."

"And what about the other ports? Monte Cristo, for example?"

"Now and again she'll serve the same purpose."

"Port-au-Prince?"

"As well as New Scotland to the north and the capes to the south. But understand that trading in a British dominion requires a somewhat different approach. I mean, there are still a few of His Majesty's subjects with aversions to dealing with rebels."

Until now they had been seated, obliquely facing a window with a view of anchored vessels: privateers from the Leeward Islands, packets from the Carolinas. But shifting to the opposite end of the room, Grove found himself examining another print of some West Indian village under swaying palms and an active volcano.

"So we're discussing trading with the enemy," Grove finally said.

"Yes, Matty, we are now discussing trading with the enemy."

"Which is done only for financial gain?"

"Oh, I suppose that one *could* argue that we all profit in some manner or another . . . but yes, the motivation is largely financial."

"And those English houses that supply the goods? Their concerns are also primarily financial?"

"Yes."

"So British arms consigned by British houses are delivered to our shores so that we can shoot down British soldiers . . ."

"Yes . . ."

"While our side's monies delivered into British houses are then taxed by the Crown in order to pay those same British soldiers?"

"Matt, you're looking at all this from the wrong perspective, through the eyes of a Continental agent. You need to see it through the eyes of a merchant, who considers war a financial arrangement between mutual interests."

At this point Grove's attention had strayed to a painting, an extravagant oil: *The Sale of Eumnaeus into Slavery*.

"I'm not here to make such distinctions, Robert."

"Of course not. You're a hunter—"

"I'm concerned about the point at which a financial arrangement with the enemy also becomes a military arrangement. Or to put it another way—at what point does one cease to deal only in cannon and musket and begin to deal in strategic, seditious intelligence?"

"I can't help you, Matty. I'm not even too sure what it is you're getting at."

"You maintain that in spite of hostilities certain English merchants have continued to conduct a flourishing trade with various American merchants, a trade that includes the sale of arms that's to our military advantage. I then maintain that in the course of this trade another sort of bargain has been made—the sale of secrets to England's military advantage. And to put a cap on it all: Colin Smith and Jane Dearborn were cut to little pieces for having discovered it."

"These are formidable charges—"

"But not unreasonable ones. I mean, if certain gentlemen in our community have established financial ties with the enemy, it's hardly inconceivable that at least one of them has crossed the thin line into treason."

La Salle cocked his head. "Soldiers have also been known to betray their fellows, as have planters and lawyers."

"The facts don't suggest a soldier, they suggest a merchant."

"Then you had better be damn sure of what you're doing, Matty, Do you hear me now? I'm speaking as a friend. This is dangerous ground you're on. A treacherous garden . . ."

Matty Grove . . . a trespasser into an exotic and treacherous garden. The analogy partly sprang from the fact that only gentlemen of great means could afford pleasure gardens, particularly within the boundaries of the city, and many of these gardens had been seeded with profits from overseas trade.

It was into such a garden that Grove was scheduled to meet the acknowledged king of foreign merchants, Robert Morris, though this particular garden belonged not to Mr. Morris but to his lesser-known partner Thomas Willing. Nevertheless it was an extravagant place with tubbed orange and lemon trees, Lombardy poplars and yellow jasmine, exotic vines cultivated from cuttings supplied by Thomas Jefferson. There was also a lovely whitewashed pavilion where Morris and Grove actually met.

It was about eleven o'clock in the morning. Morris had only just concluded meeting with various members of the state assembly in a drawing room, and four carriages still stood in the yard. The garden, however, was deserted except for a young girl tending roses. Despite a formidable reputation, the merchant initially appeared as a modest figure seated at a wrought-iron table. His clothing was plain, a simple suit of brown corduroy, his hair only lightly powdered.

It began with to what do I owe the pleasure of this visit, though Morris had obviously known for some time what Grove's business was about. Next there was oblique reference to others of the merchant community Grove had questioned—then down to the matter at hand.

"They tell me that you suspect a traitor among us," Morris said. "True?"

"There have been indications, sir."

"But no more?"

"Not yet."

"So you toy with us in hopes that one of us will inadvertently reveal something? Is that the game? I'm no longer a public man, Mr. Grove."

"So I'm told."

"Indeed, I find public life exhausting, not to mention frustrating. Consequently I now serve in an entirely private capacity—"

"Purchasing British arms?"

"Supplying General Washington with what he needs to wage this war."

"And how do you know what it is that the general needs?"

"I am kept informed."

"By whom?"

"By whomever the general decrees. You are not the first one to condemn me for having made a profit from this war, Mr. Grove."

"But I'm not concerned with your profits, Mr. Morris. More, I think, with your power."

"And how do you perceive my so-called power?"

"I'm not sure yet."

"But you intend to find out . . ."

"Yes."

Morris moved to the edge of the pavilion, drawn by the faint strains of a harpsichord. Hedgerows trimmed in imitation of a French design suggested walls of seashells.

"Regardless of what you've been told about me, Mr. Grove, personal interests aren't my only motivation—"

"Even when trading with British houses?"

"Especially when trading with British houses. Your General Washington requires arms while the British require tobacco. It's not a political arrangement, it's a financial—"

"But politics can hardly be avoided. After all, we're at war with England."

"We're at war with the king and a handful of ministers. Beyond that I would say that the majority of responsible Englishmen do not support their nation's effort here."

"And so conspire to undermine it?"

Morris withdrew a handkerchief, pressed it to his lips. "I do not think you understand, Mr. Grove. These are delicate questions. Certain British houses supply us with arms, yes. And in return we supply them with tobacco. But these mere facts do not necessarily tell the whole story—"

"Then what's the whole story?"

"I can only say that this is not a common man's war."

"There are those who would disagree with you."

"Then they are wrong. This is a war between the privileged by birth and those privileged by achievement . . . which is to say that it's a war between ruling classes, and any man who thinks differently is a fool."

"Then there are a thousand fools in this city alone," Grove said.

"Exactly, there are a thousand fools." The handkerchief replaced, Morris began to examine a rose. In his attempt to pluck the thing, it fell to pieces. "Let me tell you something, Mr. Grove. Although you may think me to be an enemy I am not.

It's merely that I tend to see this war from a different perspective than you . . . let us say a broader perspective."

"And what does one see from the broader perspective, Mr. Morris?"

"A broader struggle."

"For freedom?"

"For free trade. An international college of financial interests struggling for the right of free trade—"

"And this international college, it includes British houses?"

"As well as French and Dutch, Spanish and American—"

"Whom do they own their loyalty to?"

"To themselves."

Another rose picked too roughly had also disintegrated in Morris' hand, then at last he had one intact—a lovely hybrid from a Bourbon strain.

Grove watched in annoyance, decided to cut through. "Do you know who is responsible for the White Swan murders?"

"No."

"If you did know, would you tell me?"

"I will tell you this. Despite all our talk of revolution, it is still money that makes the world go around."

"Which means?"

"That there is likely more to this affair than either of us imagines. Indeed, it may not even be a case of treason at all. It may simply be another form of revolution. Perhaps a revolution within a revolution?"

It was noon by the time Grove had finished his business with Morris. There were, however, a few parting words along a path to the forecourt, and another brief encounter with a creature from those rarefied gardens.

It began with the appearance of a coach in the yard and the arrival of a gentleman and a woman. By way of explanation

Morris said that the gentleman was not only an occasional associate but also a formidable merchant. It was the young woman, however, who would cap the day.

Apparently arriving for an appointment with Mr. Willing, the gentleman vanished into the house leaving the woman to amuse herself in the garden, but on spotting Morris and Grove on the path she approached without hesitation. She was a most attractive figure in beige silk, face slightly rounded, eyes and hair dark against a fair complexion, features slight, reminding one of a beguiling child. Grove guessed her age at about twenty, possibly younger. She was introduced as Miss Nancy Claire; yet when Morris then attempted to introduce Grove she said that she was already well-acquainted with the investigator through his reputation.

"And what reputation would that be?" Grove asked.

"Only one that would normally follow an officer in your position. After all, haven't you been employed to save us all from that ghastly White Swan phantom?"

It was the word *phantom* that Grove fixed on, since it was new and particularly apt. Yet when he questioned her about it he merely responded with a vague smile, "They call him phantom, sir, because he is said to possess unearthly powers."

"And what powers would those be, Miss Claire?"

She returned to Morris. "Well, for example, I've actually heard it said that he has the power to pass through locked doors and solid walls, all the while toying with his victims before murdering them."

"Toying with them?"

"You know, like a cat might toy with a mouse. Pursuing and retreating, appearing and disappearing, leading one down blind alleys only to suddenly vanish again." Turning then a cat's grin on Morris: "But, of course, one can't believe everything one hears, can one?"

The Traitor

As soon as the woman had left them alone again Grove asked who she was. Morris merely smiled. "Didn't you find her attractive?"

"Who is she?"

"The mistress of another merchant you should probably add to your list of suspects—Edwin Hyde. Know him?"

"No."

"Well, inasmuch as she was undoubtedly acting on his instructions just now, I assume that he certainly knows you. Good day, sir."

Of course from then on it seemed that everywhere Matty Grove went there were suggestions of a clever phantom lingering just out of sight . . . sometimes pursuing, sometimes retreating, continually leading one down alleys only to vanish again. On one occasion, returning from a rendezvous with Tallmadge, Grove was once more reasonably convinced that someone had dogged his footsteps from across the Moore Fields to the public lamps on the Broad Street. Yet twice on turning back he found only shadows playing against the cobbles.

And also from these peculiar days: another supposedly accidental encounter with that exquisite Nancy Claire. Although nothing of obvious significance was said the smile could not have been more suggestive of some amusing secret. As she spoke, however, her eyes kept nervously straying to her master's profile in the window of a waiting coach.

chapter
twelve

A change at this juncture. It involved the peculiar Arthur
Monk and those sixteen coded pages retrieved from the courier's
leg. It was by now a Wednesday, with continually shifting winds.
Grove had risen with the first light, but remained inactive until
noon. Then he once more returned, unannounced, to the cryptographer's room.

He found the man seated on an oriental rug amid strewn
papers, assorted dictionaries and the remains of several meals. In
place of those cherished maps, the walls were now hung with
three charts or tabletures. Transcriptions of the original text had
been assigned a numerical value according to its frequency of
appearance. There were further lists of likely vowels, but only

three complete words: HIRAM, ABRAXAS, CALIBAN. There was also a small quantity of cider, which the cryptographer had apparently been consuming both for nourishment and inspiration.

He did not look up when Grove entered. Indeed, for a moment he hardly even acknowledged Grove's presence. Then absently sweeping a hand to the walls: "As you can see I've made some progress."

"I was under the impression that the matter would have been resolved by now." Grove wanted to apologize for his burst of frustration.

"It is, to a degree." He laid aside a beaten ledger also filled with a spider's web of notations. "Tell me, are you fond of hunting wild game, Mr. Grove?"

Grove shrugged.

"No? Well, nonetheless, one must learn to view all this in terms of a hunt. For example, I may not have actually seen the beast, but I believe I'm onto its scent."

He got to his feet, a slightly ridiculous figure with ink stains on his clothing, unruely hair and falling stockings. "I suppose I should warn you that we shall undoubtedly never fully comprehend the message, not without obtaining the book on which those relevant portions were based. I mean, how can one possibly unlock a door without a key?"

Grove drifted to the far wall, and to that first curious diagram that looked like the plan of some complex fortress. "What about the rest?"

"Apparently an alphabetic substitution, but I won't know for sure until I've completed the frequencies. Take these vowels, for example. Naturally one would expect to encounter them far more regularly than the consonants, but one can't always depend on it, particularly if some secondary device has been employed."

"And has it?"

Monk wet his lips. "I don't think so."

Moving to the opposite wall, Grove began to examine the most obvious signs of progress: HIRAM, ABRAXAS, CALIBAN.

"Proper nouns," Monk explained, "judging from their position in the text. The first appears only once. The others appear throughout."

"And what do you suppose they mean?"

"Hard to say. Hiram and Abraxas may be Hebraic, and naturally Caliban could be that tempestuous monster. Beyond that I can only speculate."

"Then speculate, for God's sake."

A moment's pause, the cry of an oyster girl from below, then returning to his seat on the floor: "It's more an impression than anything else, you need to understand that."

"I *understand.*"

"I don't expect to have anything of substance for at least another eight or ten hours. But if you want an opinion, I'll give it. We are not dealing with some ordinary message concerning the movement of troops and so forth. On the contrary, this appears to be some formal document . . . a contract, if you will."

"Between two parties?"

"Possibly even more. And these figures here . . . not part of the code at all but sums of money. Quite great sums of money, at that." A moment's pause to withdraw another ledger: "There also appears to be a curious symbology at work."

"What sort?"

"I'm not certain. Possibly Egyptian, possibly Druidic. At any rate it's not intrinsic to the cipher but works independently . . . as a sort of code within a code."

"A secondary message?"

"In a sense, yes."

"To whom?"

"I told you . . . I shall need at least another ten hours, Mr. Grove."

"Very well, another ten hours, then."

The Traitor

* * *

It was nearing six o'clock when Grove returned to the Dwarf. The child was nowhere to be seen. Her uncle was engaged with a disreputable widow who looked vaguely like Miss Nancy Claire . . . without the beguiling smile, of course. Talk in the tavern mainly centered around rumors of another mutiny involving two hundred men of the Pennsylvania line. It was said that the officers had been shot. In terms of the broader story, however, this evening might again be seen as a closing stage—the rear column, having completed the turn, was now prepared to commence battle.

For a while, at least until the supper hour, Grove busied himself with earlier papers: a letter from Tallmadge to Jane Dearborn inquiring about the state of British morale, Miss Dearborn's reply regarding a critical shortage of firewood. Finally acknowledging that these hours ultimately belonged to the cryptographer, he lay down to sleep.

Actually Mr. Monk did not begin to apply himself until well after midnight, and then it was a relatively prosaic process—calculating the frequencies and positions of characters, attempting to determine a reliable sequence. Next, isolating those characters most likely representing the letters *a* and *o,* he turned to the problem of consonants. Finally, as if running a hand along a darkened wall in order to find a door, he began the tentative reconstruction of words. By this time it was the afternoon of the second day, and exhaustion was clearly beginning to slow the advance.

It was an afternoon with a particularly damp mist in the lanes. Rumors of a new and deadly fever introduced by French mariners kept a number of citizens off the streets. There had also been rumors of diseased mice, which in turn had infected the cats. Consequently Grove and Monk were left in relative privacy in a coffeehouse at five o'clock.

They had arrived here independently: Grove first, then his cryptographer. Although it was not especially cold, Monk had on a heavy coat, high stock and gloves. Beneath the coat he carried another beaten copybook and dictionary. Having removed the coat and laid the copybook on the table, a plain woman brought them coffee—a southern blend laced with indigenous chicory.

Monk began as before with a brief apology. It should be understood, he said, that a cipher was like a song heard in the wind. Although one might make out certain key notes, the melody might still remain unrecognizable until one drew closer to the source. He also said that a ciphered message was like some metallic object viewed through ten feet of water—continually appearing to change shape. Consequently, he concluded, at this stage he could only offer a *sense* of the thing.

"And what does this *sense* of it tell you?"

"It tells me that this is a highly unusual affair."

"Could you please be a bit more *specific?*"

Monk shrugged. "I only know that this is not a common case of treason—not by a long shot."

"Then what?"

Another shrug. "Cabal? Conspiracy?"

The copybook had by now been laid open to a random page. Among tendrils of obscure calculations three words had been underscored: device, craft, architect. Then on a following page, Grove found two more possible decipherments: *notwithstanding* and *vanity*.

"It's all still conjecture," Monk continued, "but there are an inordinate amount of pronouns in the text."

"Suggesting *what?* Couriers? Go-betweens?"

"Confederates, I'd say."

On yet another page Grove found the word *plausible* not only underscored but circled as well.

"Let me put it like this," Monk said. "Normally one would expect to see this sort of affair in a linear fashion. That is, the traitor would stand on a thin line of deception between two warring camps—his actual loyalties in one, his apparent loyalties in another. Naturally we might find dozens of permutations, but essentially it's a linear configuration."

Grove shook his head, turned to another page: *stone, cloven foot* and *seeds of jealousy*. "And this one isn't? Linear, I mean."

"I don't believe so. I see it more as circular . . . or to be precise, a series of concentric circles like planets around a sun. Yes, there's a traitor in our midst, but at the moment it's my guess that this traitor may have several lesser allies."

"And you base *all* this on the fact that there are an inordinate number of pronouns in the text?"

"I told you, it's only a notion at this point. You're certainly not obliged to accept it."

Among the latter pages of Monk's copybook Grove found more than a dozen fragments of partially deciphered sentences. His eyes, however, only fixed on two: *Between a temple and wilderness. Insofar as our greatness is at stake.*

"How accurate do you say these are?"

Monk glanced at the page in question. "Passably faithful."

"And how long to decipher the rest?"

Another glance at succeeding pages. "I'm not certain, it seems that more than one code has been used. In fact, several."

"So the deeper you go the more complex it gets. Is that it?"

Monk let his eyes fall, a small fist pressed to the cheek. "That's exactly the case. The thing is demonic, and I mean that literally."

"Demons, Mr. Monk?" First phantoms, now demons.

"Or at least some claim to arcane powers. Take that word Abraxas, for example. I can't believe it was included arbitrarily."

"Meaning?"

"That it's to be clearly associated with various unorthodox rites—a sort of incantation. The text contains at least a dozen references to certain Druidic themes, which would seem to be relevant."

"To an overall understanding?"

"To those murders." A hesitation for emphasis, a momentary meeting of the eyes. "Look, the Druids were priest-kings, and said to have immolated victims by cutting them open. They were additionally said to have possessed unique and magical powers."

"Such as passing through solid walls?"

"As a matter of fact, yes."

"I see. So we're hunting a brood of black magicians, is that what you're trying to tell me?"

"No. I'm saying that this is a *very* unusual affair, and we would do well to bear that in mind at all times."

They left the coffeehouse together, following a warren of lanes. Mist still lay in pools along the lower alleys. Most windows remained shuttered. Although a sizeable moon had risen above the peaked roofs, the night was quite dark. Only the less reputable taverns were still serving: The Jolly Tar, The Silent Woman, The Broad Axe.

"Incidentally," Monk said after a lengthy silence, "it would seem that the reference to Caliban almost definitely concerns your murderer."

Grove at first said nothing, his attention still drawn to the ends of the lane. "And Caliban was a monster . . ."

"An *obedient* monster. Elsewhere, however, there's a more ominous reference to Demogorgon."

"What's that?"

"The infernal power of the ancients. The name alone was said to have caused death."

"What is the point?"

"No point, possibly. I just thought the reference interesting. After all, Demogorgon is a very obscure diety."

"Thus our traitor is an educated Satanist? Is that the implication?"

"I would see it more in terms of theatrics—a carefully directed masquerade to inspire fear and obedience. Which, of course, is another way of saying we're not facing a common traitor."

They had reached the Front Street by now, and a view of the moorings. Although the fog had receded the narrower lanes were still obscure. There was also, Monk was saying, the whole matter of the ciphers themselves . . . Grove had stopped listening—his head cocked back at an angle, his left hand withdrawn into his coat.

"Let me ask you something," he said at last, "if you were this traitor, how would you deal with us?"

Monk hesitated, watching Grove's eyes. "I'm afraid I don't understand—"

"Would you try to arrange our murder, or only have us closely investigated?"

"Well, I suppose that depends—"

"On what?" The gaze now turning to an adjoining alley.

"On a number of factors—look, what are you suggesting?"

"That someone is behind us right now—following us right now."

Then, although Grove stayed calm, his pistol appeared—withdrawn very suddenly, as if from thin air.

chapter
thirteen

There were still a number of unlit lanes above the Front Street at this time, extensions of earlier cartways dividing the larger lots. On the whole this was a foul district of cramped shops and tenements that had sprung up in a haphazard way. Packs of dogs ran in these quarters, as did litters of pigs. The worst lanes were infested with rats drawn by the uncollected refuse.

It was in such a lane that Monk found himself now. He stood, as Grove had instructed, in the dark recess of a bakery. His left hand, tight across his chest, held the copybook tucked beneath his coat. His right hand held Grove's reluctantly accepted pistol. Although his view extended no further than the blackened wall of an apothecary's shop it was easy enough to imagine Matty Grove and a murderer stalking one another through this warren of alleys.

For a while Monk forced himself to concentrate on tangible concerns: rats along the ledge, the stench of an open sewer, the damp chill. Then on hearing the echo of footsteps, he could no longer keep his mind from it: the White Swan killer was finally about to show himself.

When Grove had left Monk at the mouth of the alley it had been obvious from the man's eyes that this was the moment he had been waiting for. His movements had been unusually quick and precise—fingers of the left hand incessantly tapping against the thigh.

Grove's eager confidence did not inspire Monk—his back now literally against the wall, hand growing numb around the butt of the pistol. And if he had to run . . . his weaker leg had never functioned well in damp weather, and his eyes were all but useless in the dark.

Grove, on the other hand, had always seen well in the dark. Nor was he worried about the damp or the vermin or this maze of lanes. He couldn't imagine a better place to meet the White Swan beast.

He moved slowly, keeping to the shadow of a wall that descended from the stalls where Monk was. The second pistol had been loaded and primed, but he had decided on the dagger, now held loosely in his right hand. There were faint sounds from adjoining lanes: dogs or pigs rooting among the refuse, the wind stirring loose handbills, the steady tap of dripping water. Then again, from one of the lower alleys—a short series of steps.

He paused, not so much listening as mentally extending himself out across the blackened expanse of cobbles. He slid a little closer to the wall, where the littered straw and vegetable stalks would help to silence his own steps. He removed his cloak, tossed it aside, moved forward again. Shadows of a figure at the end of the lane—tall, bent, watching from the doorway of a glovery. Closer up, it became plain the figure was holding something in his hand.

A direct attack was tempting, but Grove kept to the wall until he reached a secondary passage between a chandler's shop and the lower arcade. There were shards of broken pottery but he managed to move soundlessly, keeping to the balls of his feet. From the lower arcade he moved to another recessed passage, paused. Apart from the breeze, he could actually hear the bastard breathing.

He lunged out of the passage, across the lane in a single step, threw himself at the figure in the doorway, struck with a boot to the groin, heard a winded moan, struck again with an elbow to the jaw. As the head snapped back exposing the throat, the face also became plain—a drunk, a common drunk like hundreds of others in this city.

For a terrible moment Grove thought he had killed the poor fool. Then noting the obvious life signs, an even more terrible thought crossed his mind—the killer had led him here intentionally, knowing that all men look the same in the dark, and that while he was engaged with this pitiful drunk, Monk would be left alone.

Hearing the footsteps, Monk remained still. It's Grove, he thought . . . Grove back from a search to say that it had all been a mistake; to say that this Thursday-night phantom had turned out to be some weary fool returning from a tavern. He moved the pistol level to his waist, then felt foolish and let it fall again. He took a small step forward, still saw nothing, took another. A shadow on the wall. He whispered Grove's name, then again, louder—*"Mr. Grove?"*

For a disjointed moment Monk caught a glimpse of a Matty Grove he had never seen before—a jovial fellow gliding forward to embrace a friend. But as the smile spread to a lipless grin, Monk also caught a glimpse of the blade—broad and triangular.

He was left with several impressions as the blade descended: the pressure of a hand on his wrist, his pistol clattering to the cobbles, Grove shouting from the end of the lane, a scent of burnt leaves, then again the glint of triangular steel as the blade arched into his belly.

Next he was mostly aware of the impact, lifting him off his feet. There might have also been the crack of a rib, or else the blade had snapped off deep inside him.

He collapsed slowly, fixing on the killer's eyes. Although the blade had broken at impact, at least eight or nine inches remained —more than enough to slit a throat. Suddenly, though, the killer seemed hesitant, not concerned but hesitant as Grove appeared at the mouth of the lane. Then finally turning, he loped off down the adjoining alley.

Monk lay still: left arm numb from the fall, the right still pressed to his wound. He was surprised that the pain was minimal, he'd heard that one rarely suffered in the end—and then an amazing revelation . . . *I'm not at all dead, hardly even grazed* . . . He sat up, slid a hand beneath his coat and withdrew the copybook. There may have been blood, but actually through the leather binding and some two hundred pages of handwritten notes, the blade had barely broken the skin.

He was still seated on the cobbles when Grove arrived. A handkerchief applied to the wound had effectively stopped the bleeding. The copybook that had saved his life lay between his knees. Although Grove's questions were plain enough it took a while before Monk could manage a firm response. Then finally sliding the copybook across the cobbles: "It would seem that I was exceedingly lucky."

Grove knelt to examine the wound, then the copybook—the tip of the blade still protruding from the binding. "I don't suppose you got a look at him."

"Hardly. Barely."

"And then?"

Monk shook his head. "I don't know. He's very agile, quick."

"What about his clothing? Did you notice—"

"I'm sorry."

By this time Grove had succeeded in prying the tip of the blade from between the pages. Then, although Monk refused even to look at the weapon Grove could not get enough of it.

The fragment of the blade was a triangular wedge of steel approximately two inches from base to tip, another inch across. The cutting edge was razor sharp, suggesting a surgical instrument. Precisely why it had broken was not immediately obvious —whether from some imperfection or else merely the angle of the strike.

The fragment now lay on the table in Grove's room. It was the cusp of dawn. Monk had gone to an adjoining room to try to sleep. Tallmadge had arrived moments earlier. Two sentries had been posted in the yard below. The girl and her uncle had been briefly disturbed by the voices but finally had gone back to their beds.

At first Tallmadge's interest had been drawn to the blade. What degree of skill did Grove suppose it would have taken to manufacture such a weapon? What did Grove suppose the overall length to be? Then Tallmadge wanted to know the specific sequence of events. At what point had Grove noticed the killer's presence? Why hadn't Grove pursued the man? Why hadn't he at least managed a parting shot?

Grove said that he'd have had to have been there.

"You did *see* him, didn't you?"

"Briefly, for a moment."

"And?"

"Tall, broad at the shoulders, and definitely not an aborigine."

"But no flames issuing from the mouth, no stench of death?"

105

Grove smirked, shook his head. "Actually it's more like the odor of burnt leaves, and very distinct."

There were soft cries from the adjoining room, then another uneasy silence. Although Monk had at first appeared calm, he had obviously been badly shaken.

"Incidentally," Tallmadge said abruptly, "why do you suppose he went after Mr. Monk? I mean, what could he have hoped to—"

"I told you, I think he's determined to prove himself better than I am."

"And is that how I should explain all this to His Excellency?" Tallmadge moved to the cupboard, found only empty bottles. "Look, Matty, His Excellency is under great pressure to see this matter resolved."

"And I'm not performing as expected?"

"There have been some complaints, yes."

"From whom?"

"I was not told."

"Robert Morris and company?"

"I don't know. I know only that there have been suggestions."

"What sort of suggestions?"

"That another approach might be more fruitful."

Grove took a deep breath. "Why don't you tell me what's going on, Benjamin?"

"What do you mean?"

"First you advise me not to concentrate on the murder but on the force behind the murder. Now you seem to be advising me in the opposite direction—so what *is* going on?"

Tallmadge turned to the window. "As I said, there have been pressures, uncomfortable pressures from people who worry that this investigation may now be going too far." He turned to face Grove with an uncharacteristic smile. "Simply because a man may have certain financial irregularities connected to his service, it doesn't mean that he's a traitor."

"And simply because your White Swan monster has broken the tip of his weapon, it doesn't mean he's now disarmed. Do *you* understand? The murderer is only the instrument. Catching or killing him won't end the threat. And it could cool off the trail."

"Don't you think I know that?"

"Then let me proceed—"

"By all means proceed . . . only I think it might be wise to stay clear of the more intangible elements . . . at least until we've achieved some small victory."

"There's nothing intangible about a traitor."

"Nonetheless, certain people you've been interrogating—"

"Which people?"

"I don't know. Nancy Claire, for example."

"I've hardly interrogated the woman."

"Still, she's not one to approach casually."

"On account of her relationship with Edwin Hyde?"

"As a matter of fact Edwin Hyde is a rather substantial force—"

"How substantial?"

"He has important friends."

"And money?"

"If you like."

"Which he acquired through overseas trade?"

"The man is a merchant, yes. But that's hardly the point—"

"That *is* the point. Edwin Hyde is as potentially guilty as the rest of them. And his lady—if that's the word for her—may very well know something about it."

Tallmadge picked up the tip of the blade from the table, began turning it over in his hand. "Matty, at this juncture, I feel that there are other avenues that might prove fruitful—both politically and tactically. For example, do you recall that I mentioned a rumor involving a certain rifleman from one of our West Country regiments—an unusually savage fellow with a series of similar murders to his name? Well, it happens that there may be some truth to it all. I found it interesting that this particular regiment is not unknown to you. I believe you actually served with the commander for a time—Nathan Tarr. Now Colonel Nathan Tarr of the Second Pennsylvania Rifles."

"I won't be diverted, Benjamin."

"I'm not trying to divert. I'm only suggesting you pay the man a visit. Agreed?"

"All right, I will pay the man a visit, and also follow up on other matters."

Tallmadge stayed at the table with that jagged fragment of the blade in his hand. "It doesn't seem an ordinary knife, does it?"

"No,"

"More like . . . some sort of tool. Something for a garden, maybe. You didn't happen to note the overall length, did you?"

"I told you, it was very dark, and he was moving very quickly."

It was dawn by the time Tallmadge left, almost noon when a carriage came for a pale Mr. Monk. Although patrons and residents of the Dwarf were never told what had happened that night it wasn't long before the various comings and goings stirred up new rumors—at first that there had been another murder, then that a suspect had been apprehended. After traces of blood were discovered, it seemed evident that Matty Grove had somehow once again failed.

Even the child began to lose faith in him, or so Matty Grove imagined.

chapter
fourteen

Matty Grove, as promised, did take up Tallmadge's lead about Nathan Tarr and on a Friday afternoon found himself in the Highlands again, his destination a wooded glen once held to be the domain of witches. (A pond, deep among the taller elms, was supposed to have been their final resting place.) More recently and credibly, there were said to have been bands of Hessian deserters living in this region, as well as the remnants of a lost Welsh brigade.

It was late in the day when Grove neared the glen. Along the way he had seen scouts watching from the high ground, but no one approached until he sighted the American encampment. Then he found himself surrounded by a dozen Light Horse, each man armed with the coveted French carbine. Closer, Grove noted further signs of unusual abundance: wagons laden with whiskey and powder, fattened cattle. The commanding officer's residence, a requisitioned cottage, had been particularly well-appointed.

The furnishings—a low settee in Florentine velvet complementing armchairs and a tooled draw-table—had been imported at no little expense. There was a bottle of claret and a bowl of hothouse fruit. If Grove so desired there were apples from a local orchard. In contrast, Grove's host, Nathan Tarr, was a gnarled figure—a tall, broad-shouldered man of forty-three years.

Although never exactly friends, Grove and Tarr shared memories from three unhappy occasions—Bennington, Brandywine and the route from Long Island—and it was these memories that formed the basis of their opening conversation. Next, responding to a casual question, Tarr talked about his current mission—an assignment involving the ever growing fear of mutiny. Then, without directly broaching the subject, Grove laid the tip of the murderer's blade on the table.

"So. You've gotten into the game. Welcome."

"It's no game, Nathan. The man once served under your—"

"Yes, yes, but it's only a piece of a larger, more complex situation. I've been charged with protecting a nervous Congress against a potentially mutinous army. You've been charged with tracking an improbable butcher three hundred miles from the British lines. General Washington continues to flirt with a French child, while Gates prepares to lose the South—"

"Nonetheless, the man once served under you."

Tarr poured a second glass. "Yes, he served under me."

"What was his name?"

"Dawes. Corporal Dawes."

"Christian name?"

Having drained the second glass, Tarr poured a third. "Had no Christian name, just Corporal Dawes."

"Where did Corporal Dawes come from?"

"From hell . . . Matty, let me offer some small advice. Don't pursue this matter. Walk away from it."

"I don't suppose you now know where I might find—"

"Matty, *listen* to me. This isn't your fight."

"Oh, I think it is."

"Why? Because Washington has ordained it?"

"Because the bastard tried to kill me."

They retired to an inner chamber substantially more primitive than the first—rough plaster and exposed beams, a trestled table and armless chairs. A low door led to a scullery, a window looked out to clusters of black oak and ghost vines. Tarr had brought the claret but left the rest. And now Tarr began to draw the picture that would include Corporal (no Christian name known) Dawes . . .

It was the winter of '78—Washington brooding at Valley Forge, the British encamped in Philadelphia. This story took place between the high country and the low.

It was a season of small engagements. Having mustered a contingent of two hundred men, Tarr had been charged with harassing British foraging parties. Now and again there had also been cattle raids, but mostly Tarr's efforts had been offensive, and for these he had attracted the more aggressive recruits: bachelors from the hill country, riflemen with a grudge, angry paupers with nothing left to lose. Toward the end of December came Corporal Dawes.

His age would have been about thirty, Tarr said; his height average. Complexion and hair were dark, features common enough. Some would claim that his back had been scarred from the lash, but at first sight only his eyes set him apart from the others—being particularly piercing. The man tended to keep to himself. He was a phenomenally accomplished marksman, Tarr said, which was something else Grove would do well to remember.

At the outset, Tarr went on, Corporal Dawes had conducted

himself with no more apparent savagery than any other attached to the regiment. His favorite weapon had been a Pennsylvania rifle, beautifully tooled with the head of a woman cut into the stock. More than once he had used this weapon to bring down horsemen at two hundred yards, while stationary sentries had been hit at even greater distances. He was also a patient killer, known to remain silent and motionless for hours until a target presented itself. On one occasion he had even spent a night beneath the carcass of a mule in order to dispatch a particularly loathsome officer. Thereafter he had been treated with a fair amount of respect, which in no way improved his disposition.

The first indication that all was not right with Dawes came around the end of February. Following an encounter with seventy-five fusiliers, Dawes and a party of twelve had broken off in search of stragglers. Although no one had actually witnessed what followed, several members of the party saw the bodies—three horribly mutilated bodies that Dawes had left in a wooded dell below the main British encampment. According to the most objective reports, Dawes' victims had been dismembered. The skulls had been crushed with a club, but not before the scalps had been removed.

The next incident took place some three weeks later. Again there were no material witnesses, but a number of men once more said they'd seen the bodies—two dragoons from the Queen's Rangers suspended from the limbs of an oak—throats and bellies slashed, ears and tongues cut out. At this point several members of the regiment began to object to Dawes' treatment of the enemy, saying they worried that there would be British reprisals. Tarr, however, believed that his men had been scared by Dawes and wanted him gone. The corporal's off-duty behavior had also grown more disturbing by this time. It was his habit, for example, to stay seated for hours at a time, eyes fixed on nothing that anyone could see. It was also his habit to retain some trinket from each victim: a lock of hair, an index finger, a polished knuckle bone . . . these all kept in a satchel sewn from a human scalp.

After yet another mutilation, several members of the regiment took it on themselves to have a word with Dawes. Although it was never broadly known exactly what was said, Dawes was, indeed, gone in the morning. A very half-hearted attempt to retrieve him led nowhere. Subsequent rumors of his death at Monmouth were never proved.

Tarr said that regardless of how one felt about Dawes one couldn't help speculating about what it was that drove him to such savagery. There were those who claimed that some incident in the man's past had left him deranged, and pointed to the scars on his back as evidence. Others said that his brutality had been precipitated by some Indian herb or concoction that the man had been in the habit of ingesting. And there were those who took a broad view, saying it was the war that had driven Dawes mad— the war and the temper of these revolutionary times. . .

It was dark by the time Tarr finished. The regiment had retired. The lattice had been thrown back for a broader view of the glen in moonlight. Almost as an afterthought Tarr had begun to describe the man's past in a general way, alluding to a rumor that Dawes had been an indentured servant and regularly abused. It was also said that the man had served time in Bridewell, or some equally notorious prison where flogging and branding were common fare.

Grove's attention was fixed on that "Indian concoction."

"Did it have a name?"

"None that I knew."

"But it was some kind of leaf?"

"Or root."

"And how was it taken?"

Tarr shook his head. "For godsakes, Matty."

"Smoked like tobacco? Chewed to a pulp?"

"I think it was smoked in a pipe, a clay pipe made for the purpose."

"And left a stench?"

"Yes . . ."

"Like the smell of rotting leaves?"

"More or less."

"And then what?"

"I told you. It turned him into an animal."

Tarr moved off in search of a second bottle. Finally laying a local cider on the table: "I'm only going to say it once more, Matty. Walk away from all this. Turn your back and walk away from it."

"What about his family? Did he ever talk about a family?"

"Dammit, Matty, the bastard isn't human. Now walk the hell away from it."

"What about a friend? Never any talk of a friend? A friend of means, perhaps? Substantial means?"

Tarr took a mouthful of cider, approached the window. A breeze had risen with an odor of coffee and tobacco, then the unmistakable aroma of charred beef.

"You know, this war needn't be a sacrifice, Matty. On the contrary, it can actually be quite profitable . . . assuming one plays one's cards right."

"I wasn't aware that a game was in progress, Nathan."

"Then you're bloody stupid." He moved a step closer, actually laying a hand on Grove's arm. "Tell the truth now. Don't you find your man insufferable?"

"My man?"

"Washington . . . well, don't you?"

"No."

"Well, I do."

"And who would you have replace him?"

The pressure of the hand stayed firm on Grove's arm. "As a matter of fact there are a number of men who come to mind."

Grove broke away, moving beyond the reach of Tarr's hand. "What's going on, Nathan? What are you doing here?"

"I told you, I've been enlisted to protect Congress in the event of a mutinous uprising."

"Under whose authority?"

"Actually there are several gentlemen who now fear Washington's influence on the army . . . not to mention his incompetence."

"And which *gentlemen* are you referring to?"

"Oh, those with an eye to the future. Don't look so shocked. Any fool knows that defeating the British is only half the game. There's still the struggle for internal control to contend with. After all, a pie can only be cut so many ways."

"And how large a piece have you been promised, Nathan?"

Tarr returned to the table and sat down. His eyes were evasive, voice suddenly grown soft—hardly more than a whisper. "I say it again, Matty. You don't need to pursue this. It's not your fight—"

"It seems your Corporal Dawes has butchered three of our people, Nathan. Apart from anything else, the man has already murdered three of our own people."

"But Dawes is not a man. He's a ghost. How do you expect to track an infernal ghost?"

Grove moved to the door, laid a hand on the latch. Behind him, Tarr had gotten up from the table. Although his eyes were still focused on the floor his voice was no longer constrained.

"Matty, wait a minute—"

"Good luck, Nathan."

"Matty, listen to me. Dawes had a woman. A whore."

Grove let his hand slip from the knob but did not turn around. "Why are you telling me this?"

"Maybe for old times' sake. Don't look a gift horse you know where."

"Which means you're as frightened as the rest of us."

"Which means whatever you want."

"All right. And where do I find this girl?"

"She used to work along the docks at a place called Lady Clark's."

"And Dawes was in the habit of—?"

"More than that. He was in love with her."

Although it was not late when Grove approached the city again, even the main roads were empty. Nor were there lights in the outlying inns, or drays upon the highway. Most homes were also shuttered, particularly along those narrower lanes where Grove had seen a murdering ghost the night before.

chapter
fifteen

Grove and Arthur Monk met in the garden house of an absent colleague. An occasional student of botany, Monk had often used these grounds to conduct his modest researches. There were three facilities designed for the cultivation and study of exotic flora, although during the British occupation much of the delicate vegetation had perished.

The main concern now centered on a particular variety of nightshade (also known as the bittersweet nightshade, but more commonly called the Jamestown weed). It was a tall, coarse, foul-smelling thing with incongruously beautiful flowers. Thomas Jefferson had formerly studied the plant and found it in abundance among the damp hedgebanks and thickets of Virginia.

It had also been examined by Dr. Benjamin Rush for its supposed medicinal properties. Traditionally, though, the plant was not medicinal but religious, and long had been associated with mysterious native rituals.

It was the leaf and seed of the plant that contained the intoxicating agent, Monk said. The overall effect depended on the dosage . . . a small draught supposedly produced a mild euphoria, a larger amount was known to induce startling visions. It was claimed, for example, that the Powhattan warriors were able to "will" their minds into the bodies of animals with the aid of this substance, while northern tribes spoke of an actual transformation. Occasionally ingested before battle, the drug was also said to have promoted extraordinary acts of bravery and a lust for blood.

In response to all this Grove asked only one question of Monk: what effect might the drug have on a man if consumed regularly over a long period of time? Might it not permanently affect the disposition? Might it not even drive him mad?

Madness was a factor, Monk said, but one couldn't discount the fantastic. There had been reports that tribesmen under the influence of the plant were capable of phenomenal feats: increased strength and stamina, the ability to see in black darkness, even an immunity to pain . . . "the theory being that the warrior, believing he has assumed the form of a particular animal, then takes on the attributes of that animal."

"And what form of animal might that be?" Grove asked.

"I imagine it's an individual matter. Some might assume the form of an eagle or bear. Others might think themselves a crow."

"What about a wolf?"

"Then we're getting into lycanthropy, which is another subject."

Until now they had been seated at a stout bench amid local vegetation. Going to the end of the room, Grove found himself among the more exotic vines. "Are there precedents?"

"Plenty. Even the Greeks subscribed to the notion. More to the point, there's also the belief that a man can effect such a change by rubbing his body with a salve—a typically foul-smelling brew that would eventually affect the brain."

"And assuming one applied the stuff on a regular basis?"

Monk shrugged. "Then presumably we'd be dealing with a regular monstrosity."

Having left the garden house, they soon were strolling through the garden proper, a poor place compared to the lavish grounds of the better estates. Still there were certain attractions here found nowhere else: junipers from the east, belladonna and monkshood.

Grove changed the subject. "Have you made any progress with that cipher?"

Monk shrugged. "I told you, the code is variable. It's going to take longer—"

"How *much* longer?"

"I'm not sure."

"A week? Two?"

"A cipher isn't an absolute. It's like . . . well, a rosebud. It unfolds at its own rate. If one attempts to apply excess force it may crumble away to nothing. Anyway, we're learning more all the time."

"Are we?"

"I think so . . . these botanical revelations, for example, couldn't have come at a better time. At least they tend to confirm earlier suppositions."

"Which suppositions?"

"Well, I dare say we can now assume that these people possess certain excessive tendencies . . . one even supernatural tendencies . . ."

A sideway glance by Grove. "I'll be seeing Dawes' whore tomorrow."

"As I said, excessive . . ."

119

The Traitor

* * *

It was ten the following morning when Grove appeared on the streets—hardly an appropriate hour considering his destination, though not inappropriate considering his business there. On reaching the house he found himself on the steps of a modest two-story dwelling between a stable and a groggery. Although no sign hung from the shingle, one only had to peer in a window to determine what went on inside.

He was met by a heavy woman in a bombazine shroud. After an introduction and preliminary questions he was escorted to an oblong parlor—an imitation of the worst Parisian salons. The panels bore scenes of Hindustan and the banks of the Bosphorus, while above the mantel hung a portrait of Bathsheba. The furnishings, largely in cumbersome mahogany and red velvet, had been purchased from fleeing Tories. The fixtures, mostly in beaten silver, had been purchased from the holds of privateers. There were etchings, a few erotic, most pastoral.

He waited a quarter of an hour before the girl appeared. She was thin and pale but not unpretty. Her hair and eyes were brown, she wore a shift and slippers, had a gentleman's ring on the index finger. Entering, she affected an air of indifference edging on boredom. Grove figured she was about twenty but old beyond her years.

"You wished to see me, sir?"

"Assuming your name is Sally Lock, yes."

"And what if it is?"

"Then I'd like to talk to you about a Corporal Dawes."

Although her eyes momentarily flickered, her voice was still composed. "What about him?"

"I understand you knew him once."

"I've known a lot of men, sir."

"But not, I should think, one like Corporal Dawes."

She got up from the lounge, drifting to a potted fern. "He used to come here now and again. What of it?"

"Tell me about him."

She ran a hand through her hair. "Not much to tell."

"Were you fond of him?"

"Of course I was fond of him. I'm fond of them all. Didn't you know?"

"How did you address him?"

"What do you mean?"

"By a Christian name? An endearment? What did you call him?"

"Whatever bloody came to mind."

"And what did you talk about?"

"He wasn't much of a talker, but then they rarely are."

"Still, there must have been occasions . . ."

She moved a step closer to the mirror, examining traces of last night's pomade. "Well, if you must *know,* I seem to recall that he talked about you . . . or at least the ones like you."

"And what did he say about us, them?"

"He hated them, what did you think?"

"Why?"

She ran a finger along the edge of her mouth. "Lot of pompous lawyers and generals thinking they know what's best for the world when they can't even wipe their own arses."

He continued to follow her movements in the glass—toying with the stem of a lilac withdrawn from a vase, running her fingertips along the hem of her shift.

"I understand that his back was marked from a flogging."

"All the more reason to hate your sort."

"What were the circumstances of it?"

"There weren't no circumstances. They just beat him to a pulp."

"For what crime?"

"For the crime of not being rich. Now why don't you just leave us be, Mr. Matty Grove of Boston?"

She sank into the chaise, folding her long legs beneath her. Her hands, however, were still restless: picking up stray threads from the hem of her shift, brushing a lock of hair along her forehead. "You'll not find him, not in a hundred years."

"When did you last see him?"

"I dunno, long time ago."

"How long? A month?"

"Longer."

"Six months?"

"Maybe."

"And what were the circumstances?"

"Weren't no circumstances. He just showed up."

"Saying what?"

"I told you, he wasn't much of a talker. Anyway, he's not what you think he is, not at all what you think. Always bringing a little something, never a harsh word in his mouth. And if he wasn't a gentleman proper he was better than half the cocks that parade around here."

She was reclining on the chaise now, and turned on her side, indifferently exposing a narrow thigh—and suddenly he thought he saw it clearly: Dawes a lean shadow in a squalid room, the girl paler beside him. On the worst nights they would have consumed cheap cider, on better nights there would have been madeira and they would have copulated until dawn.

"He was the one at the White Swan, Sally. He was the one."

"I don't believe you."

"He was also the one who stuck that peddler on the road."

"You're lying."

"He dismembered the bodies, cut them into little pieces—"

"I don't believe you, you're *lying.*"

He moved to the chaise, knelt down beside her. Although she'd turned her face to the wall the tears were obvious. "I must know where he is, Sally."

"Why? So you can slip a bloody noose around his neck?"

"So I can stop him from doing it again."

"Well, maybe he shouldn't be stopped. Maybe it's time you all learned a lesson. Anyway, even if there was a place, he wouldn't be there now."

He leaned closer, his hand almost touching her shoulder. "And what place would that be, Sally?"

"Go to hell."

"What place?"

"I dunno. Just a place."

"Where?"

"Along the river . . ."

"Where along the river?"

"Above what they call the Dog Marsh, but he's not there anymore. I tell you, he's not there."

"Does he live there alone?"

"Go to bloody hell."

She remained motionless until he had unlatched the door, then sensing his hesitation, she turned. "You hate him. You can talk all you want about your damned Revolution, but you're doing this because you hate him."

"If it's any consolation—"

"I hope he kills you. I hope he kills the whole bloody stinking lot of you."

A solitary evening spent in chambers at the Dwarf, and rain, a soft but steady shower associated with summer.

Grove was by now of the opinion that Corporal Dawes was very much a man-made monster—a frightful product of indentured servitude, cruel and unusual punishment, an impoverished life. And there was also this to consider if he was to be honest . . . Grove and Dawes were not entirely dissimilar.

chapter
sixteen

Still, he had to find him.

The Dog Marsh lay at the western edge of the city on a poor finger of land below the falls. It was filled primarily with swamp grass and flowering dogwood. The waters, quite deep, could be treacherous. From the road one saw nothing beyond the foliage and a glimpse of the river. It was only from the rise that the boathouse became visible.

It was a shabby affair, a gray and weatherbeaten shack above the mudbanks, a narrow gangplank leading to the water and a path through the grass leading to the road. From a distance and in the half-light of dusk there were no obvious signs of habitation.

It was about eight in the evening when Grove and Tallmadge

reached this place with seven militia armed as light dragoons. Having left their mounts in a rear hollow they proceeded on foot to the oaks. From here Tallmadge and Grove advanced still further into the high reeds. Although their view of the boathouse was still restricted, there was clearly a light inside.

They kept silent: Tallmadge resting on his knees, Grove half-reclining on a hip. A telescope lay between them on the grass, an instrument that Tallmadge had recovered from a Hessian officer.

Grove's concerns were tactical. It was a question of closing the distance, he said. Thereafter their advantage lay in numbers. The first two hundred yards would be critical. Taking up the telescope, Grove began to scan the lower marsh—a narrow lip of land extending from the river's edge.

"Why not let him have a first volley from here?" Tallmadge said.

"Because we'd never hit him."

"What then?"

Grove again focused upon the boathouse, then to a distant tulip tree. "We'll have to get closer, much closer."

Nightfall. One might have assumed that such conditions would have favored the killer, but Matty Grove was also comfortable in the darkness.

The accompanying militia moved in a broad line from the rise, Grove somewhat closer to the marsh. Of course there were night sounds: the gutteral twang of bullfrogs, the oscillating drone of crickets, muskrats moving through the vegetation, the wind clattering over the brow of the hill. Grove knew he couldn't count on these sounds entirely to disguise his approach, but he figured they ought to help.

A more conventional commander would have used four times the number of dragoons and kept them in tighter formation, but Grove's single line was intended to take Dawes by surprise. It also put the confrontation on Dawes' ground.

The Traitor

For fifty yards Grove's attention was mainly on the boathouse. That light observed earlier now suggested a single candle; the door was clearly ajar. There was no indication of movement, nor any sound apart from those crickets and bullfrogs—

Like some bird suddenly flushed from dense foliage, a shadow broke among the willows. For an instant Grove even thought it was a bird—quail or owl.

Then given the low velocity of the musketball, the wound appeared without any sign of impact at all. Merely one moment a young dragoon to Grove's left had been advancing steadily forward, the next the top of his skull had lifted away.

The young man at first seemed only somewhat puzzled, reflexively attempting to wipe the blood from his eyes. Then pausing with an odd glance at his hand, he toppled forward into the grass.

Grove knelt in the tall grass, pistol resting on his thigh. In response to the first shot, two of his company had fired their weapons—blindly and at nothing. Thereafter it was very quiet until Tallmadge called the withdrawal.

Grove waited until it was quiet again, then replacing the pistol, he slowly began to advance. He moved in a half-crouch, careful to keep below the level of the grass. Occasionally he was forced to step wide to avoid dry leaves or branches, but generally his progress was steady and measured.

He paused as he neared the first oak, peering over the stalks of grass, continuing to breathe deep and slow. There were three distinct shadows among the foliage, any one of which might have been Dawes'. Then noting the stirring reeds below the boathouse, Grove carefully started forward again. As he neared the river's edge the ground became damp, yielding. There was also an unpleasant scent of leaf mold and a rotting carcass—and then, unmistakably, the stench of that Jamestown weed.

A muskrat poised on its haunches. At first wary, the animal gradually seemed quite trusting, head cocked at an inquisitive angle, eyes fixed on Grove's gaze. If the creature were to suddenly bolt, the disturbance might well betray his position. If he tried to kill it the noise could be a giveaway. There they were, eye-to-eye, until turning on its haunches, the animal smugly slid back into the ferns.

The willows began stirring again. Grove slipped to one knee, withdrew the pistol, at first saw nothing—

It was virtually on top of him—a dark form exploding out of the grass, an unblinking eye above a long-barreled rifle.

Grove rolled on his side to escape the muzzle blast but couldn't escape the rifle butt descending like an axe. He took the first blow on the forearm, felt the pistol slip away with the impact, took the second blow on the shoulder, feeling the pain spread under the bone.

But he'd also managed to get out the knife from his boot, and no longer feeling, or fearing, any connection, went for Dawes' heart. He led with a quick feint, figuring that speed alone would not be enough. The feint became a thrust—slightly wide of the mark, glancing off a rib but still deep and firm.

They were in a *danse macabre,* clinging to one another, faces inches apart, eyes locked, Dawes' weight still working against the blade. Abruptly Grove felt himself flung away like a rag, though the knife still protruded from Dawes' ribcage, blood flowing. A lot of blood.

Dawes turned to face Grove, then slowly drew out the blade, tensing his jaw some but otherwise showing nothing. When he had it in his hand, he seemed intrigued with the weight, the shape of it. Then, as if disgusted with the undistinguished workmanship, he tossed it away.

For a moment Dawes seemed to consider another attack, but after wavering briefly on the lip of the embankment, apparently spent, he finally turned and stumbled down to the river's edge, entered the chilly water and waded out at a steady pace until the current swept him away.

The Traitor

* * *

It was nearly dawn before a proper search for Dawes' body could be organized, and then a number of factors worked against it: the swampy and malignant ground, the darkness and exhaustion. The banks were also steep in places and the water was deep. Eventually Tallmadge enlisted the aid of local residents to dredge the bottom, but discovered nothing.

Nor was there much of anything to be found in the boathouse. The single room was low and narrow, little more than a box. The planking was gray, bare. The windows had been crudely patched with sheets of paper, and a quantity of arms, including an officer's fusil with bayonet, was found beneath the floorboards. There was nothing with a broad and triangular blade.

"Maybe he discarded it," Tallmadge said. "He lost the tip and discarded it . . ."

Grove wasn't too interested at the moment. His arm and shoulder were still very sore from the blows he'd received. And he was cold, cold with a chill that seemed to spread from the groin. "I don't," he said, "think it's the kind of thing the man would have thrown away, regardless of the tip."

"All right, then maybe we'll find it on the body, tucked in the belt . . ."

"Assuming we ever find the body."

Tallmadge glanced up as if annoyed. "What's that to mean?"

"It means that a knife in the ribs is not necessarily fatal."

Among the ashes in the hearth were the remains of several meals: charred remnants of a tortoise, rodents, even the shank of some larger beast.

"By the way," Tallmadge said, "he didn't speak to you, did he? Dawes, I mean. He didn't actually speak to you?"

"No."

"But you did say that he looked at you. He definitely *looked* at you."

"For a moment."

"And what did you make of it?"

Grove took a deep breath, exhaling slowly through clenched teeth. "He just *looked* at me, that's all."

"Yes, but he must have shown something. Anger. Pain. Something."

Grove moved from a chair to the cot, still cradling the injured arm with no broken bones but a deep and ugly bruise. "It would seem," Grove said, "that he was mostly fixing the memory of me in his mind."

"For future reference? I don't think so, not with eight inches of steel in the gut. Anyway, have you ever tried to swim fully clothed? That alone would have been the end of him. And you didn't see him surface, did you? You looked and didn't see him—"

"It was dark."

"Just the same I'm calling him dead—dead and gone—until further notice." He moved to a window and a low bench where Dawes may have spent his evenings. "Besides, everyone is going to be very pleased. That pleases me."

He was right. It was only a matter of hours before word of Grove's feat at Dog Marsh began to spread. No corpse having been recovered, the celebration was not unqualified, but there was still much drinking and revelry amid stories of how that White Swan killer finally met his death, thanks to Matty Grove.

Matty Grove stayed apart from the festivities. Those who did see him up close attested to the fact that his clothing was stained with the killer's blood and his arm had definitely been badly injured. Otherwise he appeared unchanged—a dour figure in an officer's cloak and boots—and although several citizens sent notes in praise, he did not respond to a one. Nor was he receptive to those who approached him in the street. Indeed, apart from a brief conversation with dark-eyed Nancy Claire, he did not speak to a soul.

That conversation with Miss Claire occurred after nine o'clock in unusual circumstances. Having arrived unannounced in a hired coach, she sent word to his room by servant. Downstairs some minutes later, he found her in the coach, dressed much as she had been dressed on the afternoon of their first meeting in that garden with Robert Morris: hair piled in simple fashion, a dress of beige silk. The coach door was clearly ajar, an invitation to join her inside. For the moment, though, he kept his distance.

"I'm told you were wounded," she said.

In fact by now the arm was almost numb, and discolored from wrist to elbow.

"What do you want?"

She smiled. "Why, to congratulate you. It seems you've become our hero."

He moved closer, fixing on that mischievous mouth. "Does your master know you're here?"

"My master?"

"The merchant, Edwin Hyde."

Another smile. "Mr. Hyde is not my master, sir. He's a friend. Have you any friends, Mr. Grove?"

"I don't know."

"Well, in that case perhaps I shall be your friend. That is, assuming you'd have me."

He met her eyes again, but only for a moment. "Where is your Mr. Hyde tonight?"

She shrugged. "Actually, I've not seen him."

"But no doubt will be seeing him soon?"

In answer she turned her head to display that intriguing child-like profile with a woman's eyes. "In spite of what you think, sir, I'm not altogether at Edwin Hyde's disposal."

"Then what are you doing here?"

"I told you. I've come to congratulate you for having rid us of that murderer . . . at least temporarily."

"Temporarily?"

"Well, they still haven't found a body, have they?"

130

"No."

"Although, of course, I'm sure it will eventually turn up somewhere. Incidentally, should you ever find yourself on Fifth Street I'd be honored to serve you coffee . . . say, Tuesday next?"

"Will Mr. Hyde be there?"

A last smile, broader than those before it. "It's possible. Although given Mr. Hyde's patriotic duties he rarely has time for social calls."

"Too bad. I'd have liked to meet him."

"Oh, but you will . . . sooner or later."

Before departing she extended a hand through the window, but for several reasons, including the condition of his arm, he did not feel obliged to take it.

The
Middle Ground

chapter
seventeen

Not long after Grove's apparent victory at the Dog Marsh, young Sarah was called to account for a window she had inadvertently broken with a broom handle. The accident occurred in the tavern at about four o'clock in the afternoon of an otherwise pleasant day. There were eight regular patrons on hand in addition to the child's uncle, Drapier. A little later Matty Grove, drawn by the commotion, also appeared.

Drapier was dragging the child to the scullery, where she would again be punished. Suddenly, as usual as if from nowhere, Grove stepped into the doorway. He carried an officer's crop in the right hand, the injured left arm at his side. His eyes, thanks in part to the light, were black as coal.

The Traitor

It was then not so much what he said as the way he said it. "You can put that," indicating the shattered window, "on my bill." He waited until Drapier let go the child's arm, then turned and vanished.

Shortly after this incident an unforgiving Drapier began reminding any man who would listen that the White Swan affair was still far from over. Not only had their dubious hero failed to produce the murderer's body, he'd also failed to produce the alleged traitor. It was also Drapier's opinion that Grove was spending altogether too much time dallying with women like Nancy Claire.

Mostly, though, these complaints fell on deaf ears. Of course, there were those who continued to point out that Matty Grove was not a very likeable fellow, but at least for the moment he was Philadelphia's hero. He even became the subject of a ballad.

If Matty Grove was for the moment a public figure, he remained a private subject in young Sarah's heart. As before she generally only saw him in the mornings, and then for brief periods of time. Nonetheless, in brief exchanges Grove continued to show an interest in what others said behind his back.

What, for example, was the consensus of opinion about events at the Dog Marsh? And what was felt about the fact that no body had been found? Mostly he would pose these questions while he busied himself with papers. But there was one time when he seemed particularly intense—a warm Sunday morning at half past eight o'clock.

"Tell me, Sarah, have you ever heard talk of a Mr. Robert Morris?"

"Robert Morris, sir?"

"The merchant. Ever heard talk of him?"

"I think so."

"And what about a Mr. Edwin Hyde? Any talk of him?"

"A bit, sir."

"And what sort of talk have you heard?"

"Only that they've made a pretty packet, but not without stepping on the toes of others."

He nodded, even smiled. This child was really extraordinary. "On the loss of others?"

"Well, that's what they say, sir."

"And yet with all those injured toes about, you'd think that someone would eventually want to give them the boot, eh?"

"It would seem so, sir."

"Unless, of course, their hides are so thick that they wouldn't even feel it."

Sarah was flattered by his confidences, but beyond their brief exchanges Grove gave little hint about his thoughts. He kept no particular schedule, received no visitors, apart from the occasional messenger. Meals, delivered to his room, were scarcely touched. Empty bottles continued to appear outside his door.

But regardless of all this seeming marking of time, bright, perceptive Sarah sensed that Mr. Grove was onto *something* . . . it wasn't anything he said or did. But he had a look in his eye. She saw him as a sort of magician or alchemist who, noting secret signs, knew that secrets would soon be revealed.

It was also during this time that he touched her, briefly and gently laying the back of a hand to her cheek. A child but growing to womanhood even if nobody noticed, she shivered with the hope that it might have been a lover's touch.

chapter
eighteen

As Sarah intuited, a revelation of sorts was close at hand, though the principal figure was not Matty Grove but Arthur Monk. Still, her notion of a toiling alchemist could not have been more on the mark.

To begin with there was Monk's chambers, still filled with such artifacts as those primordial bones, relics from the western swamps and stuffed birds beneath dusty glass bells. In place of earlier word charts there were odd sketches tacked to the skirting board: crude visions of winged serpents, horned beasts, seven stars circling a crescent moon. There were also a chisel and mallet suspended from a string and a painting of a human eye peering above an Egyptian pyramid. Although the original sixteen pages extracted from the courier's pegleg still lay on the table in the center of the room, the oil lamps had been arranged so that the light fell mostly on a book—an ancient volume entitled *The Legend of Hiram Abiff*.

It was now ten o'clock of a Monday night when Grove arrived at this alchemist's cell to find Monk seated at the table with that book. A warm night, the shutters had been flung back to a full moon above the roofs. Dogs were barking in the distance. Otherwise the streets were abnormally still. Becoming aware of Grove's presence, Monk looked up to the doorway and for a moment seemed unable to focus his eyes. Then he took out a notebook with still another sketch, less precise than the others, almost as if it had been produced quickly to capture a fading impression. Still, the subject was plain enough: two new perspectives of what that triangular murder weapon must have looked like.

"It's still only a notion at this point," Monk said, "but as you can see for yourself . . ."

"You're not an artist, Arthur."

"Even so, what does it suggest?"

"What does it matter? The man and his knife are at the bottom of the river, or so people say."

"Matty, what does the drawing suggest?"

Grove held the sketch to the light, examined it from several angles. "I don't know . . . a bricklayer's trowel?"

"Almost. A stonemason's trowel. Modified, of course, to serve as a cutting instrument but essentially still a mason's trowel."

Grove laid the sketch down and picked up another: the Egyptian pyramid beneath an emblazoned eye. "You'd better put this plainly, Arthur. Very plainly."

"All right then. What do you know about the Freemasons?"

Another all-seeing eye had been sketched on the back of a shopkeeper's note.

"I know that they boast an impressive membership."

"True. And more specifically about this impressive member-ship?"

"I know that Washington claims allegiance to them."

"As does Franklin, as does Hancock and at least a dozen others. I am not implying guilt by association. I'm simply noting facts."

"As you see them."

"As they are. Matty, hear me out. You provided me with sixteen pages presumably drafted in the interests of a treasonous movement. I drew no immediate conclusions about the nature of this treason, nor even speculated. I confined myself to the text. Now, however, certain conclusions have become almost inevitable."

"I've heard that a Mason would rather die than reveal the secrets of his craft," Grove said.

"It's the substance of an oath taken on initiation."

"I've also heard that a Mason holds truth and liberty above everything else. Also true?"

"I'm sure some do."

"But not yours, Arthur?"

Monk drifted to the window, resting his palms on the sill. "Perhaps it would help if I were to give you some background. A medieval guild once composed of itinerant laborers was eventually taken over by gentlemen of a very different stamp. Why this ancient craftsmen's guild should have appealed to these gentlemen is not clear and not our concern. The fact remains that a number of locally prominent citizens are now calling themselves Freemasons."

"Including the better part of Congress."

"I told you, I am not suggesting that the entire order is involved. I believe I'm only speaking about a few—a small few—who may possibly be using the authority of the brotherhood for their own ends." He turned from the window to face Grove. "I don't pretend to understand it all, but there are specific indications . . ."

"What sort of indications?"

"Allusions in the text . . . passages concerning the Druids, for example, are straight out of Masonic lore. And the order has always claimed some connection with the occult, which is a prominent theme throughout the text."

Grove went to the table, leafing again through random notes and sketches. "I suppose you realize that I'll have to mention all this to Tallmadge."

"Then do so."

"I suppose you also realize he won't be impressed."

"My job is not to impress him. Yours, I believe, is. Anyway, there's more . . . it involves those murders and certain Masonic legend concerning the death of a mythical architect—"

"Arthur, please."

"No, hear me out. According to tradition this architect was murdered by three apprentices for refusing to reveal the secrets of Solomon's temple. Eventually the apprentices were also murdered . . . but in a very specific manner. Their chests were torn open and the vitals were thrown over the left shoulder. The mouths were filled with the stuff of the mason's trade—sand and limestone. *Now* do you get the relevance to your murders? The stomachs were cut open with a mason's trowel, and the mouths were packed with mortar. Do you understand? Recall the specifics once again of your murders. The three-sided blade . . ."

A brief silence. Monk was again seated among his notes, with a handkerchief he had moistened in a basin of water. Grove had located a small jug of cider. Although rather foul stuff (well past the mill, as the saying went), it nonetheless helped to steady the nerves. The previously restless dogs outside had also grown silent, or else moved on to prowl the market stalls. The candles had been extinguished, leaving only the oil lamps with their angular mirrors to concentrate the light on a page.

The Traitor

The particular page now in question was from a slender volume, *The Mayster Craft of Masonry.* Alongside it was a pamphlet of twelve octavo pages. Originally published some thirty-five years earlier in Frankfurt, it was this latter work that some said was responsible for the conversion to the brotherhood of John Locke, the famed revolutionary theoretician. There were also two similarly bound said to have been authored by Ben Franklin, and a letter on the subject bearing a young George Washington's signature.

For some fifteen minutes these various texts seemed to hold Grove's attention, then suddenly putting it all aside, he reached again for the cider.

"You're still not convinced, are you?" Monk said.

Another glance at His Excellency's signature, a finger idly tracing Solomon's seal. "Not completely."

"I'll try another approach. Suppose I were to say that whoever is orchestrating this White Swan affair happens to be a member of the guild. That's not to imply that his actions reflect Masonic temperament. It's only to say he somehow has managed to exploit the authority of the Order. Now, how does that cap fit?"

Grove poured a second glass. "Snug." He poured another. "The question still remains . . . what does one do with it all?"

"One digests it, one continues to examine and then digests it."

"Good, then digest it." Grove got up from the chair and moved to the door. "Except at some point you might consider sleeping —you look a wreck."

"There's one more thing," Monk said suddenly.

Grove stopped.

"It concerns that woman you've been seeing. Nancy Claire?"

"What about her?"

"Her lover is a Freemason. Edwin Hyde."

Grove waited.

"Do you recall that reference in the text to Caliban? We thought it might refer to—"

"Get to the point, Arthur."

"It seems there's a vessel by that name. A frigate. And the owner is Edwin Hyde. What do you say to that?"

"I say get some sleep, Arthur, you still look a wreck."

In spite of his skepticism, Grove couldn't disregard mention of the Masons. His opinion of the Order, he realized, was partly at least influenced by decades of prejudice and misconception. It was only some forty years earlier that Masonry had been nearly synonymous with deviltry, and several French Brethren had actually suffered death at the stake.

Also, as Grove had noted, there were indeed a number of prominent gentlemen within the Masonic ranks. Washington had been initiated as early as 1752, while Benjamin Franklin had been responsible for the revival of the Philadelphia lodge in 1749. Paul Revere, Joseph Warren, Hancock and Lafayette were all Masons; so were many of the opposing British officers. Masonic lore had it that lives of men were spared when opposing Brethren recognized some symbol or sign of the Order.

So it was a confusing mixture of apparent respectability and suggestion of sorcery, conspiracy and political manipulation that characterized Freemasonry. Masons were believed to have had almost total control over Britain's oriental trade, even employing Arabian assassins to deal with those who opposed them. And apart from these temporal powers, the Masons were said to have possessed real spiritual powers—this fostered by their own writings. Many of the texts in Arthur Monk's chambers alluded to such arcane forebears as the Nazarites, Druids, and Pythagoreans. And there was much stock placed in the notion that King Solomon himself had been a Mason.

Not that Grove was given to superstition—just the opposite—

but even rational men couldn't always be expected to view these Masons clearly.

And not to be discounted, he was by now very tired . . . which in itself could contribute to a sense of unreality. To a real vulnerability.

chapter
nineteen

Nancy Claire lived in a narrow two-story dwelling acquired
shortly after the British withdrawal. The property had belonged
to a devious Tory, had been confiscated under Continental authority, then sold to the woman. Rumor had it, however, that the
sale of the house actually represented part of a complex and illicit
arrangement between Edwin Hyde and then-military commander, Major General Benedict Arnold.

Nonetheless it was a fine house, not too rich, not too modest.
A small garden had been cultivated in the forecourt, full of
domestic roses and perennials. The shutters and trim had been
painted green in contrast to red brick. Beyond a simple foyer was
a low parlor furnished with the works of local craftsmen: a large

145

oil entitled *The Shepherd's Idyll,* for example, hung above the mantel and there were similar romantic landscapes along adjoining passages. There was also a curious portrait of Miss Claire as a child—half-clothed in oriental costume, her head raised from the pillow in some inscrutable reverie.

There was something of that look about her now: half-reclining on a daybed, her hair at her shoulders, little or no rouge. Although she had seemed composed when Grove had entered on the heels of a maid, he suspected that his arrival had caught her by surprise. A mess of correspondence appeared to have been hastily stuffed in a bureau. The fingers of her right hand still bore traces of ink. There were only three candles still burning in the chandelier, although dusk had fallen an hour ago.

"I'm so glad you could come," she told him.

"Did you doubt I would?"

"No, not really."

The maid reappeared: a clearly devoted woman of some strange origin—African mixed with Greek, or Haitian mixed with oriental. The name, too, suggested something exotic: *Nina.* Rather than that promised coffee, however, Nina carried a tray of claret.

"Tell me," Miss Claire said, "has your arm finally managed to heal?"

He looked past her to the haunting eyes in her portrait. "It's better, thank you."

"I'm glad. After all, there's nothing more tragic than a suffering hero."

"Well, I assure you I'm no longer suffering."

"Excellent. Now perhaps you might even begin to enjoy our city. Or is that not an appropriate suggestion for a soldier on mission?"

Without bothering to respond, he approached the portrait. "It is you, isn't it?"

"From years and years ago, yes."

146

"And was commissioned by Hyde, I presume."

She smiled, raising a glass to her lips. "As a matter of fact, Mr. Hyde has been like a father to me for a very long time."

"And is he still like a father to you?"

"On occasions."

He moved to examine a print of a young woman at the feet of an Arabian slaver. "Another of Edwin Hyde's commissions?"

"I seem to recall that one being purchased in France. Don't you like it?"

"No."

"Well, a number of people do seem to find the theme objectionable . . . which is to say that they find the subjugation of human beings distasteful."

"You don't?"

"Not necessarily. Or rather I find some forms of subjugation much less distasteful than others. For example, at least the common slave knows that he is a slave and can learn to accept it. Most of us on the other hand don't even know we're enslaved and so spend our lives straining at the shackles. And *that* is pathetic."

Until now she had still been reclining and largely hidden in the shadows. When she finally got to her feet, he caught the full view of her beauty: the raven hair, the gray-green eyes, that sense of knowing innocence.

"Now tell the truth, Mr. Grove. Don't you find the concept of slavery just a little exhilarating?" Accompanied by a mischievious cat's smile.

"I don't understand, Miss Claire."

"The absolute possession of another human being . . . say, a woman. Don't you find the notion tantalizing?"

"No."

"Well, of course, but then you already hold an extraordinary amount of power in your hands. You hold the power of life and death. Yes, I'm afraid you do." She drifted back to the window and drew the drapes. Whatever definition she may have achieved

147

in candlelight entirely dissolved in moonlight. "Now tell me something else. Do you honestly believe that this Revolution of yours will lead to anything of value?"

Her eyes, however, were still bright.

"I suppose that depends on what one considers to be valuable."

"Liberty, for instance. Do you honestly believe that a people can achieve liberty through a revolution such as this?"

"I have my hopes."

"That's where we part company, because I don't believe that anyone will enjoy liberty as a result of this war. Indeed, I don't believe there is anything at all to be gained by it—except perhaps a profit for those shrewd enough to take advantage of the circumstances."

"Such as your Mr. Hyde?"

"Yes." She stepped back from the window to face him again. "And in case you haven't realized it, your General Washington is the supreme fool for believing that he directs this war when in fact he's only a puppet like the rest of us."

She returned to the daybed, once more lost in the shadows. "Forgive me, Mr. Grove. I'm not usually so disagreeable. The fact is, I've had a difficult day."

"Indulging the whims of Edwin Hyde?"

"Actually Mr. Hyde is very understanding, except when he's angry."

"What does it take to make him angry?"

"Disobedience." She did not smile when she said it.

"And so you always obey him?"

"Almost always."

Along the far wall hung one more print of young slaves in a yard. This time the subjects appeared to be boys bound together with ropes about their necks.

"By the way," she said abruptly, "do you really suspect that Edwin is responsible for those White Swan murders?"

Grove still faced that odious print. "It's crossed my mind."

"Because he's capable of it, you know."

"I gathered that."

"The problem is, how does one prove it? And having proved it, how does one survive to tell about it? He is, after all, an extremely dangerous man."

"So they say."

"Even, I think, as dangerous as you . . . although in a different way, of course." Then suddenly rising to her feet again. "Come, let me show you my lovely garden."

It was a beautiful evening with a lingering river mist. A nearly perfect moon showed between peaked roofs, and a scent of new blossoms was on the breeze. For a while they walked in silence, maintaining a proper distance. Then at last she slipped her arm through his, his elbow against her breast.

"You find Edwin detestable, don't you?" she said in a half-whisper.

"I've never actually met him—"

"Still, you've seen enough to form an opinion. Anyway, I can see it in your eyes. You're well on the way to hating him. Not that I hold it against you. After all, Edwin has managed to cultivate dozens of enemies over the years."

"Why do you suppose that is?"

She shrugged. "Jealousy, I suppose. The petty jealousy of those who have less than he. On the other hand, one must not forget that for every enemy he has at least two friends—honorable friends."

"Such as Mr. Robert Morris?"

"To name only one, yes."

"And these friendships, how are they made?"

She turned, possibly with the first trace of real indignation. "He doesn't buy them, if that's what you mean."

149

"No, that's not what I mean. I mean, does he cement these friendships with kindness and generosity, or with mortar and a mason's trowel?"

A slowly breaking smile, a hand almost coming in contact with his cheek. "Oh, now I understand. You're interested in those sorts of entanglements. Well, all I can say is that you'll have to ask someone else about it. I'm not privy to those mysteries."

"But you have some opinion."

She stopped, hesitating, finally drawing close enough to toy with a button on his tunic. "My opinion, Matty Grove, is that you are obviously far more serious about Edwin Hyde than I had thought. Yes, you're very serious about him."

"And does that worry you?"

Both hands slid up to his shoulders. "On the contrary, I find it exciting . . . but also dangerous, which is why I think you had better leave now."

Her hands, however, had still not left his shoulders. "Yes, I definitely think it best you leave now" . . . and gradually rose to meet his lips.

chapter
twenty

Early the next morning Grove returned to the Docks, and to the commercial house of Robert La Salle. It was a warm day capped with gray clouds.

On arriving at the trading house Grove was immediately ushered into the well-appointed antechamber where rare Dutch coffee was served. Five minutes later Mr. La Salle himself appeared with an equally rare brandy. As on their previous meeting the early talk was about the past and humorous incidents from La Salle's previous career as a spy. As he spoke, La Salle more or less posed with a costly gold watch in hand. His fiery red hair was luxuriant, his pale skin had an almost porcelain glow.

On hearing the name Edwin Hyde, however, he looked sick.

"Don't misunderstand me," he said. "I'm not ungrateful to the service, nor forgetful of all that was done for me. At the moment, however, I'm a businessman, and not immune to financial attack."

"I only want to talk about him, Robert."

"And the savage only wishes to trim your hair with his tomahawk."

"They say you know him."

"Knew him. I don't now."

"Then tell me about what you knew about him."

La Salle moved to the window with a handkerchief pressed against his forehead. Then returning to the table he sagged to a chair—one of the imitative Chippendales. "Look, why don't you look at the record? If you want to investigate Edwin Hyde then look at the damn record."

"The record is only a sketch. I was hoping for a portrait."

"Then go to Morris. Go to Laurens. Go to someone with walls around his castle." He kicked at the skirting board. "Because in spite of the trappings, this is actually a delicate house."

There were two new acquisitions amid those previously noted West Indian prints—mosaic miniatures of Versailles in a summer's twilight. Grove pretended to study them before addressing La Salle again. "By the way, it was Paris, wasn't it, where you and Hyde originally met?"

La Salle frowned. "Listen to me, Matty, regardless of how one personally feels about Edwin Hyde he's generally well-liked. He is also a patriot of some stature and a gentleman. He does not make a convenient target. Indeed, he has a nasty habit of returning fire with accuracy."

"I don't intend to fight a duel."

"I was never close to the man, I can only offer impressions—"

"Anything will help, Robert."

"And I certainly cannot afford to lead you by the hand. I'll

indicate the road but that's all. After that you're on your own
. . . and you'd better watch your back every step of the way."

It was at this point that a generous amount of brandy was
poured, and the door was bolted.

Robert La Salle's story did indeed begin in Paris. It had been
quite a season, La Salle said, a time of politics and love. Arriving
the previous spring of '74, he had ostensibly come to learn the
tobacco trade under the tutelage of an uncle from Virginia. This
uncle, however, was not a businessman at heart, "and at seventeen years old I was even less inclined to think in terms of profit."

It was mostly a social time. The days began late, rarely before
noon; then generally lasted until three or later in the morning.
Although their lodgings on the road to Versailles had not been
lavish, they afforded one the pleasures of both a country and city
existence . . . one could leisurely pass long afternoons in the
gardens and yet still arrive in plenty of time to dine at the better
salons. There were also, of course, the brothels to be reckoned
with, and one could not overlook the palace if one hoped to make
any headway within royal circles.

Frivolity and luxury, romance and infatuation were the staff
of his life, said La Salle. "For a while I was in love with the
daughter of a certain Madame Brillon," he added, "but eventually found that I preferred the father's wicked mistress. Meanwhile my uncle had become involved with a young lady-in-wait-
ing. There were a number of concurrent delicious political
schemes, and I was regularly mistaken for Thomas Jefferson,
probably on account of the color of my hair."

It was in the context of this rarefied world that Edwin Hyde
first made his appearance. He was accompanied by an exquisite
girl of about twelve who was, naturally, taken for his daughter
or niece. The child, however, was not a relation—she was the
young Miss Nancy Claire.

The Traitor

At first Hyde and the child resided at an unappealing hotel on the poor side of the river. "Of course, I only knew the place from a distance," La Salle said, "but even from a distance one could not disregard the stench." The surrounding lanes were no less offensive with the continual clatter of iron wheels and cries of vendors. This was also one of those districts where the cobbles were thick with a viscous black filth that devoured the hem of a person's clothing.

Still, this was the hotel that Hyde first came to. His assets were negligible, his prospects dim. His main haunt at the time had been a squalid groggery where sea captains met and devious bargains were made. He saw no women as far as anyone knew, and literally kept the child on a leash for fear that she would be stolen.

Had Mr. Hyde's fortunes never improved, no one would have ever heard of him. . . . "We were, after all, still quite a select society," La Salle said. The ambitious Edwin Hyde's change of fortune involved a strain of sugarcane newly introduced to French plantations in the West Indies. Referred to as the Bourbon cane, it was supposed to have yielded four times the amount of sugar as previous strains. But it demanded a good deal more labor to cultivate, which placed great stress on the backs of slaves.

In fact, the slave trade had never been very profitable. For one thing the cargo was too fragile; one could lose half a consignment to a virulent fever, known as the flux. The Negro was susceptible to an inflammation of the eye, which more often than not left him blind, and there was always a certain percentage of those who took their own lives and those who just died of melancholy. Procuring a willing and able crew was another problem, and an experienced captain could cost a small fortune.

Yet given this urgent new need for slaves created by the Bourbon cane, handsome profits were suddenly earned in a relatively short period of time. Of course, the trade still had its inherent liabilities, but if ever there was a profit to be made with human cargo, then Hyde was the man to make it, La Salle said. He never allowed his captains to pack the hold so tight that the flow of air became constricted. Nor did he tolerate undue abuse, which, he discerned, tended to break the African's will to live. His Negroes were fed with a mixture of rice and yams, their water was sweetened with molasses. All ships under Hyde's commission had to employ surgeons to treat the Negroes, and the captains received bonuses for each slave delivered to port in good health.

There was another overriding factor in Hyde's success—he loved the business. "Now, of course, there were very few in the community at this time who openly opposed the trade on moral principles. But it is one thing to condone it, quite another to relish it . . . and Edwin Hyde most definitely came to relish his role as a slaver."

"And what was Hyde's age at this time?" Grove asked.

"About forty five."

"Which would put him just above fifty now?"

"A vigorous fifty, make no mistake about that."

"Do you happen to recall anything at all of his personal habits?"

La Salle shrugged. "He was ordinary enough in most respects, although they said that for a time he ate no meat and drank only light wines."

"What about his personality?"

"Charming . . . when circumstances called for it."

"Which were generally the circumstances in Paris at that time?"

"Not necessarily," La Salle said. . . .

Although there were less than three dozen foreign merchants regularly conducting business in Paris at that time, La Salle said, competition was often fierce. Rivals might find themselves facing pistols at dawn. Hyde, of course, had never been the sort to lay his life on the line for a few thousand livres. He also wasn't one to let another get the better of him.

"From what I could gather," La Salle said, "his tactics were usually subtle. A small sum paid to the shipping authority, for example, could effectively keep a rival's vessel delayed for weeks. Assets, unless entirely liquid, were also subject to constraints. Then too, dealing with native brokers could be quite tricky, while Edwin was apparently the master at playing both sides against the middle in order to starve a competitor. And need I add that he was not above hiring some broad-fisted cove to drive a point home?"

It was about this time, La Salle went on, that Hyde fell in with a circle of like-minded merchants who called themselves the Internationalists. "Now, there were a number of select societies gathering in private salons about town to forward some particular philosophy or science. These so-called Internationalists were cut from a different cloth. They were pragmatists, wholly concerned with practical day-to-day power."

La Salle said that their loyalties were "flexible." Their voice was not loud at Versailles but commanded attention. They were men of action. Although their stated aims were free trade and world harmony through commerce, they were known to be a self-serving lot, given to rougher stuff as well—at least one unhappy fellow got himself squashed like a grape.

But it was a comparatively minor incident that most came to mind whenever La Salle heard the name Edwin Hyde. It happened on the island of Jamaica some eighteen months later. "I had sailed from Charleston to secure a consignment of salt on behalf of a Boston house," La Salle said. "Enroute to the leeward side of Statia, I suddenly found myself in a depressing waterside room above the docks at Kingston. The weather, as usual, was abominable. The women were either poxed or difficult."

On the morning of the third day, however, La Salle rose from his bed, flung back the shutters and was greeted with a remarkable sight: a dark woman in white seated on a finger of black rock below his window. Her eyes were either fixed on the blue-green horizon or else on a blue-and-red bird perched among the saw-

tooth palms. For a long time he was transfixed. Finally, fetching an eyeglass he had purchased in Montego, he was met with an even more surprising vision; this enchanting beauty on the rocks below was not a woman at all. She was the child Nancy Claire.

"Very well, I thought, Mr. Edwin Hyde is in port. No reason to be concerned about that. Yet I was concerned . . . although I wouldn't have been able to tell you exactly why at the time."

It was not until the following morning that La Salle actually met up with Mr. Hyde. He had decided to spend it in a leisurely way on the veranda of a portside café where local merchants often met. "But after less than an hour I heard a commotion from somewhere down the land. I joined a small crowd of similar layabouts, made my way past a small cane field, and there encountered a singularly disturbing sight: the herding of some eighty Negro slaves into a latticed pen."

They were a pitiful sight, La Salle went on. Although some effort had been made to bathe and clothe them, many were still naked and covered with filth from the hold. There were a number with those horrible wounds caused by the shackles. To make matters worse most were very young, not more than twenty. About a third were female, and at least a dozen were hardly more than infants. Once they had been led into the pen and secured with ropes about the necks, two gentlemen appeared: a notary or factoring agent, and the royal administrator. The slaves were then measured against a wooden marking rod and summarily examined for signs of what the Spanish called the black vomit.

"After about a quarter of an hour," La Salle continued, "I noted the presence of a third gentleman. At first I took him for another factoring agent, and from his clothes a wealthy one. But then noting the authority he commanded, I realized he must have been the owner of every unfortunate soul in that pen. And on seeing his face I realized that it was Hyde."

At first, La Salle said, Hyde seemed mainly concerned with some problem of accounting, because he continually kept referring to a small ledger. "Eventually, however, it became clear that the real object of his interest was a girl. That is, a female slave of about fifteen or sixteen years. Uncommonly pretty even in her present condition, she was tall and lean with that coppery complexion one normally associates with the noble tribes. Her neck and shoulders were particularly well—shaped, her features were strong but not indelicate. Although wearing only a brief rag that hardly covered her thighs, she possessed what I can only call a rare dignity."

She was standing third in a line of seven, La Salle said, and Hyde moved along the rank until he came face-to-face with the girl. Then he casually tore her garment away, leaving her bare.

There was an extraordinary silence at this point. The girl, too, remained motionless and still, La Salle said, her eyes did not waver for an instant.

Then as if responding to her challenge, Hyde placed a hand on her breast and began to examine the nipple. He did this without the slightest expression of desire, but rather like one might test the teat of a cow. From the breast, he slid his hand up to her lips . . . "at which point, much to my pleased surprise, she bit him. Hard. Drawing blood. It was magnificent.

"God only knows what then must have passed between them as they continued to stare at one another. It seemed one of those supremely pregnant moments when anything might have happened. Unfortunately, the man has never possessed a shred of real subtlety, and so simply had her flogged. It lasted, I suppose, about five minutes; and as I said, the expression on his face was unforgettable—so much more than mere satisfaction."

After that, La Salle said he only saw Hyde on the odd social occasion: funerals, the second Independence celebration, weddings. (It was not long after this incident that Hyde was himself married to a certain cousin of Madame Leray de Chaumont. Yet, of course, it was all for convenience and he had rarely seen the poor woman since.) "Still, in fairness, a number of gentlemen counted Edwin Hyde a friend, and several prominent women have found his relationship with that little Nancy Claire . . . charming."

And what was the nature of Hyde's relationship with Nancy Claire? Grove asked.

A distant glance to that mosaic of Versailles in twilight, then: "To put it bluntly, the man owned her. He literally owned her —lock, stock and barrel." Although not yet noon, the heat had grown oppressive. "I'm not sure what else I can tell you," La Salle said. "I pretty much lost track of the man after the war, and as I said, I rarely see him now."

"Does he still trade in slaves?"

"Occasionally, but he's hardly the only one."

"And about Miss Claire, what was the arrangement?"

"Nobody knew for certain, but apparently she had been the intriguing end of a bargain made in Ireland. Either that, or he won her at the gaming table."

"And his intentions toward her?"

"I told you, she was exceptionally attractive even as a child."

By now Grove had embarked on a slow tour of the walls. There were two more etchings reminiscent of an early life in Paris: poplars in moonlight, moored boats on the banks of the Moulin Joli.

"Incidentally," Grove said suddenly, "did the society that Hyde belonged to have another name?"

"What?"

"Those Internationalists, did they have another name?"

"Legions of hell. Devil's brigade. I don't know."

"And no other affiliation?"

"What do you mean?"

"They weren't, for example, also associated with some larger movement . . . say, the Freemasons?"

The Traitor

La Salle turned with a slow smile, a hand poised on his hip. "Oh, so that's it. Well, my God, Matty Grove, now you're in a pretty mess."

"They tell me that Hyde is a member, Robert, an enthusiastic member."

"Likewise your bloody Mr. Washington. Look, you're by no means the first to walk this road, Matty. In fact I'd imagine that at least a dozen have walked it before you. And they've all ended up as laughing stocks . . . or worse."

"I'm merely putting the question, Robert. Is it possible that the Brotherhood is a factor?"

"A factor? No, it's not a factor. It's a damn morass, and you'll not be the first to sink up to your neck in it."

Having completed his tour of the walls, Grove joined La Salle at the window. Given the heat and the brandy, they were both perspiring heavily.

"Far be it from me to dissuade you from any particular course of action," La Salle said, "but I'd not fool with those Masons until you know more about them. You should also bear in mind that Edwin Hyde has more than a single pair of ears and eyes."

"Meaning?"

"That if you continue to question people about him it won't be too long before he hears of it . . . and I suggest you stay away from Nancy Claire. She's not exactly what she seems."

chapter

twenty-one

More rain and a wind that was out of order in July. The highway was deserted. The dozen dragoons from Tallmadge's escort waited below in the public room. Although this inn lay only six miles northeast of the city, it had taken Grove all morning to get to it. There had been no consolation beyond salt pork, bread and rancid butter.

"Are you aware that Edwin Hyde has singlehandedly raised the better part of two regiments?" Tallmadge said. "He's further been unusually generous to Congress."

"Would you have expected anything less?" Grove replied.

"What do you mean?"

The Traitor

"We aren't looking for a British spy, Benjamin. We're looking for a patriot who has turned sour."

The room was low and narrow with rudimentary furniture. The window looked out to a stable yard littered with wet straw and muck. A dog slept beneath a cart. In addition to the cider there was a Spanish claret called tent, also foul-tasting.

"I don't suppose you find it meaningful that Hyde has gone to great lengths to secure French and Dutch funds on our behalf," Tallmadge said. "Nor has there ever been any indication that the man has been less than forthright when dealing with the army commercially."

"And why should he have been less than forthright? It's not his plan to *cheat* us. He wants, I think, to bury us."

"With his Mason's trowel?"

"I told you, that's only a notion at this point—"

"Arthur Monk's notion?"

"Partly."

"But you also believe it has some merit, correct?"

"I believe it's worth exploring."

"In the interest of incriminating others?"

"In the interest of determining motive and means."

Tallmadge faced Grove. "Has it ever occurred to you that if all this Freemason business were true, His Excellency would have noted it long ago?"

Grove turned to the rain-streaked window. "Perhaps he has noted it but kept silent for other reasons."

"Such as?"

"I don't know. To protect the integrity of the Order."

"Well, I can't accept that."

"Can't you? Benjamin, listen to me. If we know anything at all we know that this is a complicated affair. The issue isn't just one man's treason, it involves, I think, a dozen, two dozen men —a nest of them."

162

"And Edwin Hyde sits on top of them all like a brooding hawk? It strikes me as thin."

"And Monk's observation about that reference to *Caliban* as the name of Hyde's vessel?"

"Also thin. Look, I don't say you're wrong, only that an accusation at this point would be premature."

"I agree."

"Then why are we having this discussion?"

"Because I will soon be moving on Hyde and I thought you'd like to know it."

They parted in the carriage yard just as the rain had begun to slacken. A cow, too, had emerged from its shelter, the steam rising from its back in the cold air. Although Tallmadge's dragoons had continued to wait patiently in the public room, one of them had begun an air on a hornpipe. It was an old tune, and the words, if they had been sung, would have told of some Highland sorrow.

"Incidentally," Tallmadge said at last, "I may soon be meeting with an acquaintance of yours who might be of some help with that Masonic theory."

Grove ran a sleeve across his mouth—still the taste of a foul meal. "What are you talking about?"

"Apparently one of your Boston compatriots is arriving this evening to petition me for a favor. In that he's also an enthusiastic Brother, I thought I might persuade him to speak with you—as one favor for another."

"And exactly who is this Boston compatriot?"

Tallmadge shook his head. "Let me speak with him first."

"But you believe that he'll—"

"Let me have a word with him, Matty."

By now the rain had died to almost nothing, a thin mist on the wind. As if in response the hornpiper had begun to play a livelier tune.

163

The Traitor

"I hope you'll take no offense," Tallmadge said suddenly, "but I do feel obliged to ask. I mean given what's at stake, one can't help asking—"

The stable boy had appeared and Grove had already begun to prepare himself for the road. "Ask what?"

"About your . . . motives."

"What about them?"

"Well, I can't help wondering if your suspicions toward Hyde aren't in some way related to your feelings toward Miss Nancy Claire."

"And what do you suppose my feelings are toward Miss Claire?"

"Well, I don't know . . . but it's beginning to worry me."

Regardless of what Tallmadge may or may not have sensed in that stableyard, there was most definitely a change in Matty Grove at this point. It was not the sort of change that a casual observer would have noted. Indeed, Grove himself was hardly conscious of it.

Young Sarah, intuitive as always, sensed it from the start, and was both frightened and pleased. Although she had been asleep when Grove returned to the Dwarf that night, she was so accustomed to his footstep that she immediately awoke and slipped on her gown. Then although she spent only a moment with him in the corridor, the change could not have been more apparent.

At first he faced her from about a dozen paces. His boots, uniform and cloak were still damp from the road. His holster, pistol and horn were slung across a shoulder. Although the curtains were obviously swaying with a draft from the chimney, it almost seemed as if Grove had brought the wind in with him— a churning mass of air beneath his cloak. It was also unusually cold.

"What's your trouble, Sarah?"

The voice, too, might have been something from out of the wind—distant and hollow.

"No trouble, sir."

"And no devious schemes afoot?"

"Sir?"

"What's your uncle been up to?"

"Mostly in the counting room, sir."

"Well, let's hope he's not counting on my good graces, eh?"

"Yes, sir."

Thereafter, without knowing why, she tended to see him as a hungry cat that has finally spotted his prey in the distance. The body keeps stock-still, the tail swishes, the claws not yet extended but the upper lip risen to reveal fangs.

It was also about this time that the excessive drinking stopped, and she only rarely heard him pacing the floorboards in the dead of night.

chapter
twenty-two

The Boston compatriot referred to in conversation with Tallmadge was Paul Revere. The circumstances of their meeting was
no mystery. Although the silversmith still enjoyed a degree of
fame for his premonitory midnight ride, he had lately fallen into
disrepute for his role in the Penobscot expedition. (Specifically,
he had been charged with negligence for failing to rally his
command in the face of a British assault.) So his presence in the
area was rightly assumed to be connected with his efforts to clear
his good name. His brief involvement with Grove, however, was
based on an altogether different matter that would never become
public knowledge.

To put it bluntly, it was Revere's secret life as a Mason that ultimately brought him into this affair. Although not yet a driving force in the Brotherhood, his was an influence to be reckoned with; and was to be particularly remembered for having led his fellow Brothers on the night of the Boston Tea Party. He was also, more to the point, no mean scholar of Masonic lore—hence Ben Tallmadge's earlier remarks in the stableyard, hence Revere's subsequent meeting with Grove . . .

They met in a remote place some fifteen miles northeast of the city—called the Widow's Rock after some local legend of betrayal and murder. It lay on a kind of bluff above broad woodland. The adjacent cliffs were steep and treacherous. The tortuous path was hardly better. A deep pond fed by subterranean streams lay at the base of the knoll. The surrounding oaks, supposedly cursed by a witch, were stunted and gnarled.

It was very nearly twilight when Grove and Revere came together here. The shadows were dark among those twisted oaks, and the hollows were scarcely lit at all. Although nearly forty-five years old, Revere was in many ways still a young man. He stood a little shorter than Grove but seemed to have a notable strength about him. And, of course, he remained fit from the saddle.

"I don't owe you," Revere began, "I don't owe you a damn thing."

He tended to walk with a stiff gait, speak in clipped sentences. His clothing was hardly the stuff of a gentleman: coarse britches with a broad belt, a coat with deep pockets.

"No one says otherwise, Paul."

"And that's another thing. What I'm about to tell you stays between us. I've still got a semblance of a reputation to protect."

"It's only the White Swan that I'm asking about."

"Yes, well, that's the point, isn't it? Your White Swan business goes right to the heart—right to the very heart." He glanced over his shoulder. "How much have you heard so far?"

"About what?"

"The Order. What have they told you about it?"

The Traitor

"Not a great deal."

"Just the same, put it out of your head. It's all no doubt a pack of lies, so put it out of your head and we'll start from scratch."

They sat down on a small knoll above the cliffs where nothing grew except tufted grass and a finger of moss between exposed roots. Crows called from impending cliffs. There was an occasional breeze through chasms of bare rock.

So this was the setting: a forlorn mountaintop adjacent to nothing. Revere seemed to speak in a dull tone, while Grove listened with an intensity he tried not to show. They did not face one another, generally looked off into the distance, though now and again Grove did turn an eye to the trail, on the watch for intruders.

These Freemasons, Revere said, were not an easy force to pin down. One might as well try and pin down the wind. He compared the movement to a cloud, vast and ever changing and elusive. The Brotherhood is strong, he said, because the Brothers are many and because they are an active part of the world.

Several years ago, Revere said, he'd asked a master of the Lodge how it was that the Order could stay unsullied although it conducted itself in a distinctly worldly fashion. The motive, was the answer. Which was not to say that the ends entirely justified the means, but the wise man, like God, occasionally worked in mysterious ways.

As for the deeper mysteries, Revere said that although it was difficult to trace the origin of symbols, no one could deny the ancient tradition of the craft, which presumably justified it even if it didn't explain it. Much was rooted in a morality derived from ancient Greeks and perfected by Christian revelation, a methodology coming from Egyptian masters and burnished by enlightened Jews. One also, Revere said, had to acknowledge the influence of oriental philosophies and the art of mathematics as taught in Alexandria.

168

"I suppose you'll want to talk about that Edwin Hyde now," Revere said abruptly. He said that although he didn't know the man well he was acquainted with the type . . . "Which is to say that Hyde is not the only one with schemes."

"And what sort of schemes are we talking about?" Grove said quietly.

Revere shook his head. It's no secret, he said, that a number of prominent merchants had lately joined the Masonic ranks. After all, by definition Freemasonry was an international movement, and so it stood to reason that men of international affairs would naturally see some advantage in the society.

"I don't think we're discussing a natural arrangement," Grove said.

No, Revere conceded, it was not a natural arrangement at all. It was a most unnatural and complex chain of loyalties encircling the globe. And it was not merely some economic or political movement. It was of itself another whole kind of revolution . . .

They moved along the path next to the cliff. Mistlike pools of frozen water, a bank of clouds like some advancing ocean wave . . . yet no wind, not even a breath.

"I only met him once," Revere said. "Hyde, I mean."

"Under what arrangements?"

Revere shrugged. There had been no arrangement, he said. Hyde had sort of appeared out of the blue with the strangest party that anyone had ever seen: a Venetian duke, a prince of Araby, some sort of count from Croatia. "There were also a fair number of your lawyers, and a gaggle of traders."

At any rate they had all showed up in the dead of night at a tavern called the Green Dragon. After a fair amount of revelry they proceeded by torchlight and lanternlight to what served as the Grand Lodge of Boston.

"About a score of us eventually attended," Revere said, "but not without misgivings. To begin with they'd taken liberties

169

where liberties shouldn't ever be taken. A fourth taper when the service only calls for three. A veil of solid crimson when it should be of purple and blue. No Starry Girdle of Prudence, and three or four other such transgressions."

But that really wasn't what troubled him . . . it was, he said, an unbecoming arrogance. "Needless to say we were glad to be rid of them."

"And what would it take to be rid of them now?" Grove asked.

Revere shook his head. "It's not that easy, Matty. Never was, never will be. And you can't break them outright either, not even with the whole of George Washington's army at your side."

Grove moved closer to him. "They say that these White Swan murders were based on a ritual. Is that true?"

In answer he got: "And then Solomon sent servants to the King of Tyre, saying, behold I intend to build a house unto the Lord my God. And when the architect of this house was murdered, goodly Masons were dispatched to avenge him—which they did in a manner to inspire both horror and respect."

"And any member of the Lodge would know these signs? The gutted torsos, the sand and lime . . . these would be clear?"

"Clear enough."

"Then what is the point?"

"I told you, to inspire horror and respect."

Revere stepped away, becoming a stiff figure with his right hand jammed into his pocket. Grove watched him for a moment, thinking that Dawes must have been instructed. Not being a Mason himself, he must have been instructed according to the ritual.

Suddenly Revere said: "Look, I'm not saying that there isn't something to be resolved here. I'm only saying that maybe you're seeing it all wrong. Your White Swan story may look like simple treason and murder. It's not. It's more than that."

"Facts and logic would indicate otherwise, Paul."

"Then the facts and logic are wrong . . . or else misread.

Anyway, not a complete picture. Of course, I'm just a mechanic. But I'm not lying to you. I may not understand the whole of it but I'm not lying."

"I never thought you were."

"This is a strange beast you're tracking now, and unless you see it with your own eyes, you might never believe an account of it."

"Oh, I think I'd believe it, Paul."

"Then believe this . . . it's not only the British you're fighting. You're fighting the future too. You may think these Masons are living in a misty path with their incantations and their temples, but that's just the trick of it. In fact they're the future . . . and a devious future it is, with trade routes like some spider's web from Europe to the Indies, and every merchant-monarch beholden to a banker with a tally sheet. And to hell, they say, with your glorious Revolution—this war is mostly another far-ranging exercise in profit."

They began to walk again, descending from the knoll to the deeper glade. A premature moon above those misshapen oaks tended to accentuate the terrain and the mood.

"No doubt I sound bitter," Revere said.

"No more than some others of us."

"Just the same, it's not bitterness talking. There's a new wind blowing from the east, and it smells of money."

"Does it also smell of Edwin Hyde?"

"Maybe, but he's not alone. There's a whole pack of them."

"All in league with the British?"

"Now that's exactly my point. Matty, this isn't politics. Mostly not. This is business . . . if Hyde is dealing with an Englishman then I think he's dealing with him as a partner. For profit."

"And where's the profit?"

"Where do you think? They mean to buy and sell the whole bloody world, starting with the ground beneath our feet."

The Traitor

They began to walk again, Revere at a quick and determined pace, Grove following the shadow.

"I don't suppose you know the name of the others, Paul."

"It's not the names. If you want to understand this business then look to the money. That's where you'll find the answers—in the give and the take of the money."

A final hesitation . . . "And don't go talking to anyone else from the Order. I'm not part of Edwin Hyde's circle but I just might have been."

chapter
twenty-three

Half a mile south of the Dwarf lay a stretch of road called the Cutter's Lane, a dank place with little more than a rank of butcheries and shops that no one patronized. Ghosts were said to walk this road, particularly the spirit of a girl who had died at the hands of her father. It was also said to have been a meeting place of hooligans and thieves. Not surprising, it was not well-traveled at night.

Nonetheless, since this lane was also the shortest route between the Dwarf and the city's eastern edge, Matty Grove often passed here. On the night in question it was about eleven o'clock when he entered the lane. A moon the size of a guinea had risen to the steeples. The fog had withdrawn to the river in the face of a stiff wind.

He saw the soldiers from a distance—two members of a local brigade that had avoided the worst of this war. They appeared a stone's throw east of the Dwarf. A sergeant identified himself as Mr. Hoop. His corporal was a lean cove in ragged coat and trousers. Since they were on foot and armed with cudgels, Grove first took them to be members of the night watch.

At first it was only Grove's name and the nature of his business they demanded. Then it was his pistols, and, after a search, the dagger in his boot. "Lay your hands on your head," the sergeant said, "and your heels against that wall."

Grove seemed to go along, to be overwhelmed—and then he struck, stepping in with a little spin, grabbing up his pistol and wielding it like a club. He went for the corporal first—he hadn't liked the look of the man's cudgel, a nasty length of oak with a cluster of nails through the knot. His blow caught the ribs and laid the man out like a handkerchief. His second blow shattered the man's jaw and some teeth with it. Grove turned to the sergeant. They circled, then Grove delivered one quick jab to the bridge of the nose, another to the groin.

Both men were semiconscious, but were in no condition to resist as Grove examined the contents of their pockets.

Among the items Grove removed from the sergeant's pockets were two letters from a woman named Nell, twenty English pounds and an enlistment notice from the previous autumn. These now lay on the table in Grove's room along with a bottle of port and the same pistol Grove had used to defend himself. In the corner of the room sat Arthur Monk. To Monk's left sat Ben Tallmadge. Grove faced them both from the window.

"Let's assume," he said, "that you're desperately hungry and have just discovered that a full and sumptuous meal has been laid in the kitchen. As you approach the table your foot meets a rat—a dead rat. Now, what are you to make of it? Did the creature eat off your plate and then die? Or was the death entirely unrelated? Either way, you must make a decision—to eat or not to eat."

Tallmadge spoke up first. "I suppose that depends on what has been served. I, for example, have never been able to turn down a plump capon." Then as the smile froze, "For godsakes, Matty, you nearly killed two men tonight. I hardly think that this is the time for speculative thought."

"It's exactly the time for speculative thought, because I believe my encounter with Hoop and his corporal was in no way accidental."

"Meaning?"

"That both men were undoubtedly accountable to Hyde."

"And you base this on twenty pounds in their pockets?"

"I base it on the fact that until this month both served beneath Hyde's guidon—the Second Independent Foot."

"Matty, there have been at least a thousand poor souls with the Second Foot. Anyway, what motive would Hyde have had for sicking two louts on you?"

"Oh, I think the motive is obvious," Monk said quietly from his corner. "I think it was a test, a test of will and ability."

"Well, I suppose we might as well get on with it," Tallmadge said. "I mean what's done is done, so we might as well get on with it."

Monk took out another wad of notes—a solid packet fixed with a bit of string. "Now, of course, these are only preliminary findings," he said. "The real wealth will require a bit more effort."

"I'd be happy to settle for a handful of coppers at this point," Tallmadge said, receiving not even a smile in return.

"Mostly it concerns one of Hyde's lesser known ventures," Monk continued. "The purchase of printing presses."

Tallmadge gave a sideward glance. "Printing presses, Arthur?"

"Four. Of Dutch manufacture."

"And exactly what is their function?"

"I'm not sure."

"But you're sure that they are to be used for no good . . ."

Grove spoke up. "Look at it this way, Benjamin. What better tool to sway public opinion than a printing press?"

Monk added, "There's also the matter of Hyde's relationship with Nathan Tarr and those Second Rifles. Ostensibly Tarr has been charged with protecting the city in the event of a mutiny. But what if this isn't his purpose at all? What if his purpose is to serve as Hyde's personal fist to smash all those who would stand in his way?"

Tallmadge turned to Grove. "How many times need I say it, Matty? I must have proof.". . .

There were two or three minutes when Tallmadge and Grove were alone on the staircase while Monk waited below.

"I suppose you'll be wanting to see that Nancy Claire woman next," Tallmadge said. "I suppose you're going to pay her another visit."

Grove shrugged. "It would seem like a logical step."

"You're not sleeping with her, are you?" No response. "Well, are you?"

"No."

"Because that would complicate matters, you realize that, don't you?"

No response. Only a look that could kill.

Grove's encounter with those soldiers from the Independent Foot was the talk of Market Street and still more in the taverns and groggeries. Although opinions varied, nearly all conceded that Grove may have been very close to resolving this case or very near to failing . . . but that either way the strain was beginning to tell.

They were right on all counts. Especially the last.

chapter
twenty-four

It was nine the next evening when Grove returned to the home of Miss Claire. The weather was wretched. Only the broad streets still bore signs of life. He found her, as before, composed in her drawing room: doors thrown open to that modest garden, chandelier swaying in a damp breeze. She wore another simple gown loosely pinned at the waist. Her hair was partially gathered at the neck. Her feet were bare.

He faced her in the doorway. Even after the maid had left he continued watching from the doorway. He realized he couldn't have looked worse—unwashed, unshaven and unslept—but she did not seem in the least alarmed.

"So you've returned to me."

A nice opener, however obvious. He moved to her escritoire and began to examine stray correspondence—French, Italian, British. "You sound as if you were expecting me, madame."

"Oh, but I was. Indeed, I've been expecting you for days now."

"And what prompted these expectations?"

She shrugged, toying with an ebony dagger presumably used to break the seals of her lover's letters. "Just a feeling."

Inside the folds of scented stationery also lay a roll of English currency—a good deal of it. "Tell me, madame, are you aware that there are laws against consorting with the enemy?"

"And so there should be, sir."

"There are also laws against trying to usurp the authority of Congress."

"Assuming, of course, one accepts the authority of Congress."

"No, the law stands regardless of acceptance. Also, the penalty is death."

She smiled nicely, still turning the dagger over and over in her hands. "And what, sir, is the penalty for false accusation, libel and slander?"

Slipping the money into his pocket, he moved to the alcove above the garden. Among rows of boxed lime trees stood the marble bust of a Moorish slave complete with turban and veil. "The fact is, Miss Claire, I may not yet have sufficient rope to hang Edwin Hyde, but be assured that I can slip a noose around your pretty neck."

"On what charge?"

He took out the wad of currency, let it drop on the floor. "Oh, I'm sure I can find something. After all, Mr. Hyde may be beyond reproach, but you're a liar and a whore. No, you're not so grand—you're chattel."

He managed to intercept her wrist before she could slap his face. Then twisting her arm until she dropped to her knees, he hit her twice. Hard.

She played a good scene, if a bit on the melodramatic side, he thought. She shook her head and even laughed. "God, what a stupid fool you are. What a marvelously stupid fool . . ."

She got to her feet and moved to the mirror to examine the damage. Then again under her breath, "God, what a *stupid* fool."

Why did Hyde tell you to approach me?"

"There, that proves what a fool you are—"

"Why did Hyde—"

"He did not tell me to do it. It was *my* choice to approach you. Mine alone."

"Why?" Did he believe her?

"Because I thought you might help."

Play along. "Help with what?"

"Help me be *rid* of him." She turned from the mirror. "You still can't grasp it, can you? You still fail to understand."

"Understand what?"

"That I've hated Edwin Hyde for years."

She was either very clever or telling the truth—which might make her foolhardy. He led her to the garden, a better area for confidences. It was still oppressively warm, even with a stronger breeze. The scent of fuschias was in the air and thin moss yielded underfoot.

"Here is a story about Edwin Hyde," she said. "Many years ago he purchased an African warrior to be used in wrestling matches, which at the time had been popular. This warrior seemed a formidable opponent—tall and broad with massive shoulders and limbs. Unfortunately for Hyde, the Negro lacked the will to win. Hyde tried every device imaginable to inspire the man: rigorous training, a hearty diet of red meat and corn, various native herbs said to instill a will to fight. Eventually the clever Dr. Rush was even called on to prescribe some medicinal aid . . . no use. Then Edwin had an inspired idea. He promised that should the wrestler recoup five times his purchase price he would

179

be given his freedom. Suddenly the poor fellow began to fight like a tiger, defeating one opponent after another. Meanwhile Edwin began to accumulate huge profits from bets made at these matches, and it wasn't long before he'd recouped well over five times the amount he had paid for his slave. But he always found one reason or another to keep the man in the ring. Finally, during one particularly brutal bout, the African received a terrible blow to the head. After that he got his freedom, which he was never able to enjoy except as a pitiful idiot.

"Edwin Hyde may not always be willing or able to meet a man's price, but he never fails to understand what that price is. He also has a remarkable eye for detecting the weakness in others, and once he has found that weakness he never fails to exploit it."

"And what was your weakness?" Grove asked.

She shrugged. "My youth, I suppose."

They began to walk, following one of the more neglected paths over a carpet of moss that broke like piecrust beneath their feet.

"I was, after all, only nine when Edwin first acquired me," she said.

Grove kept quiet. He'd said too much earlier.

"From a broker in Dublin. Two hundred guineas, F.O.B. London. It seems Edwin had been taken with my eyes."

"Nine . . . what did he want with you at such an age—"

"Ah, Matty Grove, you are a fool, as I said. Can't you guess what he wanted?"

He could, but he didn't want to face it. "Still, there must have been some sort of defined arrangement—"

"The *arrangement* was whatever Edwin wished it to be."

"And your parents?"

"Dead."

"Brothers and sisters?"

"All dead. I had been awarded to a workhouse, so in a way Edwin was an improvement. Was I abused? By normal standards, yes. But I was never deprived. Even during the lean months he saw to my material needs, and an education. He also at times hired women to beat me with a birch while he watched from a chair in the corner."

Her matter-of-fact tone was as chilling as her description.

"What about his wife?"

"The comtesse? Well, that was hardly an affair of the heart. In fact, I don't believe he's seen her since '76. Anyway Edwin has no interest in those he can't possess. It's his nature."

They had reached the garden's center and the bust of the Nubian slave. There were also row on row of roses, and those neatly boxed lime trees Hyde had insisted she cultivate for the fragrance.

"I don't mean that Edwin is a villian," she said, and seemed, to his astonishment, to mean it. "In many respects he is the most charming man a woman could care to meet . . . and all the better gentlemen admire him." She frowned, shaking her head and half-smiling. "As a matter of fact, sometimes I think that *I* must be the villain for loathing him as much as I do. He can have that effect on you."

"Why haven't you ever tried to leave him?"

"Oh, but I have. Once when I was ten, then again at thirteen. The first time I was caught after only two days, but the second I managed to reach the Hudson. I met a boy there from West Kerry and we lived off stolen fowl and apples. I had a cat we called Jolly Roger, and some thieving friends who called themselves the Black Boys. We dreamed of discovering some vacant island and living like savages. It may all have been impossible, but I recall that I was quite happy."

"Then why did you return?"

"Oh, I didn't. I was retrieved . . . like any runaway slave. And because Edwin has always been a traditionalist, I was then whipped . . . bound to a bedpost and whipped for three nights in a row."

They had reached the more remote end of the garden where

the path was choked with thistles and vines that had slipped from the walls.

"Have you ever thought of using the law on your behalf?"

"Don't be bloody silly. Edwin *is* the law. Besides, where would I go? What would I do? I'm a horse that has been trained to accommodate only one rider."

"Then at least try to slip the reins and learn to accommodate yourself."

"You still don't understand, do you?"

He waited.

"I mean, how it is with Edwin and me."

"Well, maybe if you tried—"

"*Listen* to me, Mr. Matty Grove. Edwin Hyde does not merely own me—he created me."

They had returned to her drawing room, where the candles were nearly spent. That ebony dagger still lay on the floor. Although the maid had retired there were sounds through the house as the wind continued to play on loose doors and shutters.

"You don't believe a word I've said, do you?" she said. "You still think I'm acting on Edwin's behalf, don't you? Well, consider this . . . if you were to murder him tonight I swear I wouldn't lift a hand to stop you."

He met her gaze in a looking glass. Although her eyes revealed nothing, her face was tracked with tears. "And is that what you would have me do?"

She shook her head. "I don't know."

"Because there may be other ways to deal with the man—"

"Such as?"

"Tell me what you know about the White Swan murders."

A short sigh. "What of them?"

"Is he behind them?"

"Probably . . ."

"But you've no proof?"

182

"No."

"Who was Corporal Dawes?"

"Another of Edwin's creations."

"Did you know him?"

"Not exactly. He'd been indentured to a planter in Virginia but proved to be intractable and dangerous. Edwin admired the man's spirit and purchased the contract for his own estates. He tended to use Dawes for all the tasks no one else had the stomach for . . . breaking limbs, cracking skulls, that sort of thing." She did not smile this time.

"How long ago was this?"

"Six, seven years. By the end of it Dawes had become an incredible creature . . . an authentic monster."

"Did you know he used the Jamestown weed?"

"Another of Edwin's experiments. I believe he first fed it to that wrestler of his, then to dogs. It killed them. Of course the good Dr. Rush was involved in all this as well . . . as the scientific advisor, I suppose you might call him. Dawes, it seemed, got to love the stuff, couldn't get enough of it."

He sought her gaze in the mirror again, but the eyes remained unreadable. "How many others were involved?"

"I don't know. A dozen?"

"And with what influence in the army?"

"I can only guess."

"Are there also links to the British?"

"Possibly. Probably."

"And how are they maintained?"

"With all sorts of devices. Letters in the hollows of trees, lanterns on top of hillsides at night. Ciphers. You see, Edwin has always been a most devious, and ingenious, bastard."

"What about the couriers?"

"Soldiers, I suppose. They would go unchallenged."

"But you've never actually seen them."

"What I've learned has been by-the-by. I'm not Edwin's

183

confidante, Mr. Grove. I'm his slave and his whore. As you said . . ."

The wind had grown capricious, alternately rising and dying. For a time she seemed transfixed by the swaying chandelier. There were strains of a tin whistle from the neighboring lane.

"Do you hear that?" she said. "There. Do you hear it? They've been at it for a month now. Not always the same piece but always one sort of lament or another. Like an accompaniment to Edwin's plots." She sank back to the chaise, tapping a finger in time to the music. "He truly does possess the power. There's simply no question about it. Edwin has the power."

"What sort of power, Nancy?" Never having used her name before, but somehow feeling that the time was right.

"I don't really know how to put it . . . it has to do with bending the will of others, with planting notions in their heads. Sometimes I can actually feel him inside of me . . . like a cold hand against the heart. Then, of course, he took up with those Freemasons, and that made it all the worse."

"How?"

She pushed up on an elbow, apparently unmindful that her gown had slipped past the shoulder. "There's a light side and a dark side to the Order. I don't know much about the light side, but I know about the dark because that's the side that Edwin has taken to. It's like a fog, it has no particular form, it's always shifting and changing. At the same time it's also like one of those octopods, with tentacles spread all across everywhere." She shook her head. "Of course, Edwin tells me that there is no such thing as a giant octopus, but I don't believe it. I think ships are lost to them all the time."

He thought he detected tears again and brought her the claret from an occasional table.

"What would you say are their aims?" he asked.

She smiled, but her eyes appeared glazed. "Isn't it obvious? They would rule, everywhere . . ."

"How?"

She slipped off the chaise to pour herself a second claret. "Did you know there's a banker in Frankfurt who holds at least three dukedoms and a prince in his pocket? Did you know that King Georgie has to beg to pay for his Hessians? Did you know that your Congress has been bought and sold by merchants who don't give a damn about liberty?" She ran her fingers through her hair. "And now you ask me how they plan to rule? It's *money*. You can forget all you've heard about kings and queens, assemblies and parliaments—they don't measure up. What counts most is a pack of money men like Edwin, meeting in secret. Smart, powerful and out of control . . . the way Edwin controls me . . ."

After a sip of the third glass she laid it aside and returned to face the garden from the doorway, and for a moment she might have been an exquisite child again, lifting her arms as the breeze filled her gown, then drifting back.

"Would you care to see my last resort?" she said suddenly. "This," and pressed a tiny pistol into his hand.

He held it up to the light, examining an inlay of ivory and black pearl. "A gift from Edwin?"

"For protection against thieves. Although lately I've come to think of it as my last resort."

"And you would use it?"

"I like to think so."

"Then I suggest you purchase something larger. This might only do a partial job."

She returned the pistol to the drawer, then moved back again to face the garden.

"What happens now?" she said so softly she seemed to be talking to herself. Then more clearly, "What now?"

"That depends—"

"On what?"

"On how far you're willing to go to stop him."

She glanced back over her shoulder. "Oh, so that's it. You

would have me be your spy. You want me to spy on Edwin. Very well, I shall do it. But it really won't change anything . . . you'll still have to kill him in the end, because if you don't he'll destroy us both."

She insisted on accompanying him to the gates. Although it was still oppresively warm, she had thrown a shawl about her shoulders. They walked in silence for the first dozen or so paces, carefully avoiding bits of windblown refuse on the path. When her shoulder finally brushed his arm she did not seem to notice.

"They say you were once an Indian fighter," she said. "Is that true?" With her hair at her shoulders, she struck him as incredibly beautiful, and desirable. "They also say no one can touch you, and that you kill because you enjoy it. True?"

"What do you think? Do I seem like someone who enjoys killing?"

"No, but then again neither does Edwin." She approached the gate, lacing her fingers through the wrought iron. "You realize that Edwin already knows about you. He knows what you've come to suspect, and he knows you've seen me. He also knows how to fight you . . . he may not be your equal with a pistol or knife, but he has other talents you can't imagine."

He moved to her side, also lacing his fingers through the iron lattice. "When does he return to the city?"

"A week, perhaps less."

"And what will you tell him when he asks about me?"

"I suppose the truth—that having formerly hunted savages, you are now hunting traitors."

"And if he asks about us?"

She drew closer, seeming to want to put a hand on his hand but holding back. "I don't know, Mr. Grove. What should I tell him if he asks about us?"

chapter
twenty-five

Shortly thereafter Grove was seeking answers to more complicated, less specific questions than the provocative one posed by
Nancy Claire.

It was a Tuesday when Grove appeared at the State House,
asking for candles, ink and paper. He was directed to the office
of a Mr. John Sully who had been responsible for congressional
folios since the British evacuation. Although some debate was
still in progress below, these remote upper chambers were fairly
quiet. The papers lay in haphazard piles along the walls of three
rooms. Some were bound with ribbons, others with bits of string.
There was more in the Council Chamber closets and still more
in the Carpenter's Hall. Grove kept to these primary stacks.

187

The Traitor

Toward four o'clock Arthur Monk came and was soon at work in a neighboring room. A wise man, Monk kept his distance from Grove and left him to burrow like some mole or hedgehog amid his mountains of paper.

Grove had said they should now think in terms of the broad picture, but in the beginning Monk could not see the forest for the trees.

"You want this whole shelf reviewed?" he had asked, referring to the first full series of congressional folios.

"Yes."

"And what is it we're to be looking for?"

"A ripple in the pond," Grove said. "A ripple, Arthur, that might denote the presence of some damned beast under the water."

Monk thought that a pretty colorful image for a man like Grove, but held his tongue.

For the first night Monk found himself on well-trod ground. There was much on the early economic tribulations, and many pages of discussions about the British squeeze. Washington generally fared well in the records, but here and there he appeared as some tyrannical demigod, John Adams was seen as a fool, Jefferson a coward and Franklin a fool.

On the second night Monk toiled amid overseas correspondence: packets from Paris concerning French aid, letters from London about British subterfuge. Nevertheless it was about at this point—a sultry Friday night—that Monk at last began to glimpse the first fruit of their efforts. A bit earlier he had gone out into the yard, which at this time was still enclosed by high walls but not yet surmounted by lamps. It was a bright night with three-quarters of a moon above the tower and a clear vision of the skyline from the steps. He had been taking a breath of fresh air for half an hour when Grove suddenly appeared at his side, in his hand portions of three letters from abroad and loose sheets of congressional minutes.

He began with the letters that constituted a report from a confidential agent in London. He did not give the agent's name, said the man had served as secretary to a prominent barrister and member of Parliament. The letter concerned the lord's debates on the course of the war, the financing of it and the politics. There were also, Grove said, enlightening passages about the king's ministers and their machinations to subdue uncooperative Whigs.

The second document was a report on British intelligence with particular emphasis on Mr. John André, adjunct to British Commander-in-Chief C. Henry Clinton. The paper seemed to give credence to Smith and Dearborn's earlier claim that André had been in correspondence with at least a dozen treasonous Americans, including an officer of prominence.

"And whom do you suppose this officer might be?" Monk asked.

"If I knew that, I wouldn't be standing here like a damn fool." They withdrew to the shadow of a gateway, presumably safe from prying eyes. Grove tore a shred of vine from the wall, laid it at his feet, and said that Monk should imagine it a line of conspiracy that favored neither the Crown nor Congress but lay in the middle ground.

"So what's your point?" Monk said, also tugging on a vine. "That this John André isn't working in His Majesty's interest?"

"No. Only that a compromise has been made. England, it seems, has come to realize that it's better to end this war with a profit than to win it at all costs."

They began to walk. "What was it you told me when you saw that packet from Clock?" Grove said suddenly.

"What—?"

"You said, I think, that the form suggested a contract, an agreement between two parties."

"It was only a guess, a notion—"

"But not necessarily wrong." A quick glance at a passing figure in the window of an assembly chamber. "For whatever it's worth, they tell me that the king's ministers are as unhappy with this war as anyone. They see no advantage to be gained, and no good chance of victory—not since the French commitment, anyway. They're also upset by the cost and the prospect of trying to keep us subdued in the years to come. The problem is, though, they also don't want to lose the colonies—that's what we still are to them. So the question for them is *this:* how do you have your cake and eat it too? Or maybe it's *and not let it eat you too* . . . Look, you said it yourself, Arthur. This isn't a case of ordinary treason. Our man hasn't sold himself to the British. He's worked out a deal. A very nasty one for us and ours."

In addition to their efforts with the official minutes and correspondence, toward the end of the third evening Monk again took out those sixteen pages retrieved from Mr. Clock's wooden leg. Only fragments of that letter had been deciphered, yet it was Monk's notion that by comparing the possible decipherments with certain crucial themes in the larger record, some value might shake loose, some vital thread from the overall knot.

"But given that our traitor seems a logical beast," Monk told Grove, "it would seem a reasonably accurate portrait can be deduced from the logical assemblage of facts."

And so he began with the most easily observable truths: the British seizure of two frigates and all cargo off the coast of Florida on the seventh of June, '77; the death by hanging of four rebel spies on the ninth of July, '78; the uncanny foreknowledge possessed by British commanders all through the spring of '80. Naturally, Monk reasoned, one could not lay all these misfortunes at the feet of one traitor, but one could not rule out the possibility that the traitor had enlisted the aid of others in order to serve his masters.

Next Monk turned to the traitor's background and specifically the six or seven years before hostilities. Of course, this was less stable ground, but after an intensive review of the records Monk felt confident of at least the following: that this traitor had almost certainly spent time in London before the war, and that he had served either as an independent merchant or a commercial agent for one of the leading houses. Also, it was Monk's opinion that the man's current relationship with the British was partly based on earlier arrangements made with those of "his own kind."

Finally, and perhaps most pertinently, Monk returned to his earlier Masonic notes and various letters regarding members of the Philadelphia Masonic lodge. Again, one couldn't draw absolute conclusions, he told Grove, but at the same time it was just about this point when he first began to refer to the traitor as "Edwin."

Hearing the name made Grove shiver.

These nights also gave Monk an opportunity to see Matty Grove as no one—except maybe young Sarah—had seen him before. Although by no means a student of the mind, it hardly required a Benjamin Rush to see that Grove was a hard man with bitter memories and strong feelings. At one point, by accident, Monk found at least a dozen mentions of Grove in the journals; each a footnote on the exploits of an unusual patriot. It seemed the man had been involved in the unofficial deaths of four British officers and members of Loyalist brigades. He was known to have fought like a wolf in the western campaigns before padding off to the secret war.

It was in such a light that Monk now tended to see Grove— as some wary wolf from the Highlands. He could at times appear tame, but one only had to observe the way he sniffed the night air or stood at a window scanning a remote horizon to know such a pose was more apparent than real.

Grove only spoke about himself once—it was eight o'clock of the third night, along the tower staircase. Earlier Monk had unearthed two letters from Tallmadge about Grove's participation in the Cherokee wars of '76. Monk couldn't help posing a question or two. He wanted to know about the Black Creek slaughter, but in fact the question lay very near Grove's personal tragedy—the death, four years earlier, of his family at the hands of savages.

"So what exactly is it you're asking?" Grove said, looking ominous with the moonlight bisecting his face.

"Well, nothing exactly . . . I was just wondering—"

"What was done to my wife and child? They hacked them to pieces, then burned what was still alive. And the gentlemen soldiers from across the ocean put them up to it."

Not long after this night Edwin Hyde returned. Although he had not yet officially resumed residence in the city, his yellow coach had been seen in the forecourts of several prominent homes. Grove had begun to sense the merchant's presence, and developed a low but persistent fever that left traces of sweat along his hairline. And deep inside his gut he hungered for the man who summed up all the evil in his life.

chapter
twenty-six

Hyde appeared at ten o'clock on a Tuesday morning. It was a gray day, luminous clouds and no definite light. Various bells had been ringing since dawn. The breeze brought a scent of the open sea. Grove had just come out of a coffeehouse below Water Street after another night in the congressional folios. Hyde's fine coach stood at the end of the lane.

On the face of it, it was another chance encounter. In truth everything had been planned: the hour, the setting, even the opening remarks.

It began with a seemingly accidental meeting with Benjamin Rush. Grove had just stepped into the lane when Rush approached from the doorway of a neighboring shop specializing in medical instruments. After a brief innocuous word or two, Rush glanced up the lane and said that *there* was a man Grove might like to meet. Moments later Hyde emerged from his coach, an imposing figure in black velvet, high stock and jabot.

"So, you are the intrepid investigator," Hyde began. "I've heard much about you."

The face was leaner than portraits had suggested, but the eyes were familiar enough.

"How do you do, Mr. Hyde?"

A quizzical glance directed to Rush. "How do I do? I do better since you've proved yourself capable of defending us, but I shall do still better once you've actually managed to kill that White Swan phantom."

The voice, too, was not precisely what Grove would have expected—high, cutting.

"You're not convinced the man is dead?"

"Of course, that's always a possibility, but from what I understand he doesn't die easily. I tend to have a feeling about this, a distinct feeling."

He withdrew a pocket watch, a modest piece with a brass fob and plain face. "Come, Mr. Grove, walk with me. The doctor is pressed for time but I have a few minutes to spare."

So they began to walk—just the two of them—moving along at a slow pace on this shabby lane.

"Tell me, Mr. Grove, has it ever occurred to you that these White Swan murders may in fact be a blessing in disguise?"

"Heavily disguised, I'd say."

"On the contrary, I think it's obvious. After all, how many otherwise irresolute citizens may have lent their support to our cause as a reaction to such British atrocities? I'd say a goodly amount, wouldn't you?"

"Well, that presumes that the British were responsible for the murders."

"Or that they are made to *appear* responsible, if you get my point."

"How does one deal with those who are actually guilty?"

They paused at a shop window displaying nit-killers, fine-tooth combs, cheap stays and ribbons. "Do you know what constitutes the first lesson of political agitation, Mr. Grove? It's this—if one hopes to sway the popular mood in a given direction, then one must bear in mind that people can't stand too much reality. Reality gets complicated. Consequently one must present them with only acceptable truths—simple and easily digestible."

"And who decides what's an acceptable truth?"

Hyde pressed a gloved hand to the windowpane, apparently interested in a rusting rat trap. "Actually there are several gentlemen I would trust with that task. Although personally I've always been partial to the works of Tom Jefferson. Such a way he has with words . . . 'We hold these truths to be self-evident, that all men are created equal; that they are endowed by their Creator with certain inalienable rights; that among these rights are life, liberty and the pursuit of property' . . . or should that be 'happiness'?"

Behind the first trap lay another device with steel jaws and a heavy mainspring.

"And what if one finds that the public rejects the acceptable truth?"

"But how can they? Particularly when it's clothed in such noble sentiments." He tapped a finger to the glass. "I wonder, do you think that contraption is effective? I'm told that my larder is teeming with mice."

Having reached the cul-de-sac, they started back along the opposite side of the lane.

"Incidentally," Hyde said abruptly, "I hear you've met Miss Claire." His face as he said it was the distorted reflection in the window of a rag shop.

"We met at the home of Mr. Morris. Does that concern you?"

"Of course not. But tell the truth. Didn't you find her charming?"

"I suppose . . ." God, how he wanted to strangle the man, there and then.

"Well, in that case let me propose a bargain. You resolve this White Swan business, resolve it well, and I shall let you have her for a night. A kind of reward, you might say . . ."

"What will Miss Claire have to say about your generous reward?"

Hyde allowed a thin smile he might have been suppressing from the start. "My dear Mr. Grove, simply because Tom Jefferson has proclaimed all people to be equal and free does not necessarily mean that it's so. Besides, she likes you, I can tell."

Later Grove was seen in the early evening at the edge of Edwin Hyde's estate, which lay to the northeast, a broad place of lush pasture and orchards. There were also acres of uncleared land where a man might have easily watched the house while keeping unseen.

Grove, however, could not have been more obvious: upright in the saddle along the main approach, his now rather famous cloak across his shoulders. At one point he was even seen directing an eyeglass to an upper window, where Edwin Hyde was also watching.

chapter
twenty-seven

The boat lay in shallow water just south of the High Street wharf. It was an odd craft with a makeshift cabin of scrap timber and bark, a stern sweep-oar and jigger. A three-pounder had been mounted on a swivel to the bow. Powder had been stored below. It was nearly midnight when Grove and Nancy Claire boarded the vessel. When she had first stepped below, cloaked and hesitant, he had felt it best to lay out a candle. Now, however, it was quite dark. Although the cabin was small, care had been taken to insure comfort: the bunk fitted with linen, leaded panes of glass in the portholes, even varnished woodwork.

"I don't suppose this belongs to you, does it?" she said.

"It belongs to a friend."

Although the cloak had been removed, her face remained in the shadow.

"I thought you had no friends."

He put a tankard and bottle of rum on the small round table.

"Do you entertain spies here?" she asked.

He poured the rum, she ignored it. "No."

"But this is a spy's boat, isn't it?"

"Yes."

"I thought so."

After briefly examining the bottle, she finally tasted the stuff. Then settling onto the bunk, she looked to the porthole. There were two sloops of war to the port, one of them damaged from a recent engagement.

"Did you know that I talked with him?"

She nodded.

"And he said he knew about our meeting. So I presume he asked you about it."

Pouring another two fingers of rum: "So what if he did? I told him we didn't talk about anything that mattered."

"And he believed you?"

She leaned forward until the thin light fell across her cheek. There were two bruises, suggesting that Hyde had struck with both the forehand and the back. "Not at first. He seemed to think I'd betrayed him. But after he was done with me, he probably came to believe it."

"Does he do that often?"

"Do what?"

"Beat you."

"Yes."

"Why?"

"I don't know, maybe he enjoys it."

Now Grove wanted to strangle her, for her infuriating calm,

and her long suffering. Lord, he was getting perverse too . . .
"What else did you talk about with him?"

A shrug. "Nothing much. Mostly he talked about his horses."

"What about them?"

"I can't remember."

"Did he say anything more about me?"

"He asked if I knew that you nearly killed two men in the Cutter's Lane. And if I was aware you once hunted savages for scalps. He compared you to a wounded animal—a panther, I think."

"And what do you think he meant by that?"

"That you're dangerous, dangerous to him."

"Anything else?"

"He asked if I found you appealing."

"And what did you tell him?"

"No." She would not look at him as she said it.

The sound of wind through taut rigging, the wash against the hull. "Where is he tonight?" Grove asked.

"With his associates, I suppose."

"Who might they be?"

"Probably those Freemasons."

"What if he decides to pay you a visit?"

"He won't."

"But what if he does?"

"Then I shall tell him that I've taken a lover."

He got up from the little table and moved past the bunk to the hatch. Two heavy Durhams were approaching—without lights and too low in the water.

"Are you sure that no one followed you here?"

She sounded irritated. "Yes, I'm sure."

"What about your servant?"

"Nina?"

"Would she betray you?"

"Of course not."

"How can you be so certain?"

"Because she also knows that Edwin's a pig."

He heard her reaching for the bottle again, then putting it down with a bang. "Look, what do you want from me?"

He turned from the hatch, pressing a hand to the bulkhead.

"Right now I want you to tell me everything you know about him."

"I've already done that."

"No, you haven't."

She reached for the bottle again but he snatched it away.

"What is it that you think we're doing here, Miss Claire? Playing parlor games?"

She met his eyes for a moment. "Why can't you just leave me be? Just leave me *be.*"

He put the bottle down, took hold of her shoulders. "Tell me about him, tell me about Edwin Hyde."

"I can't—"

"*Tell* me."

"*No.*" Shouting it as she spun away, sprawling onto the bunk. Her fingers examined a bare shoulder. "You've ruined my dress."

He looked at his hand, at the thin strip of fabric torn from her sleeve. "Nancy . . . hear me out."

She shook her head, an involuntary shiver. "Can't you see that I'm afraid of him? Can't you see that?"

He knelt at her side, whispered her name again, brushed his lips against hers. She only continued to look at him.

"He'll kill us. Don't you realize that? He'll kill us—"

He kissed her again. When he had finally slipped her dress off the shoulder, two or three more bruises were revealed. The rest was flawless.

Rain had come with a low hiss on the water. After sliding a

hand along the smooth plane of her belly he let it die on her left breast. Although more slender than he had imagined, she was no less exquisite.

"Have you any idea what Edwin would do if he were to see us like this? Have you any idea at all?"

"Listen to me," he said, making her look directly at him. "Edwin is as good as dead. Understand that—"

She took his hand, pressed it to her lips, then back to her breast. "I understand why you are saying it. I wish I could believe . . ." He brushed away a lock of her hair to see her eyes. "Maybe this will help. It's about his correspondence with Clinton and the British." She put her head on his shoulder. "There's a cottage on the edge of Edwin's estate. He calls it White Hill but it's actually in a place called Parson's Rise. There's no one living there except an old man named Jack Drum and he's more than half mad . . . but he's loyal to the Brotherhood and so Edwin trusts him." She reached for his hand. "About once every fortnight, sometimes more, little packets come through there. Edwin's even had me see to it—carry little packets of letters and such to Jack Drum's place. Usually it's done in the morning because the soldiers always come around dusk—"

"What soldiers?"

"Wait. At first Jack used to be the messenger because who would stop an old mad fool on the road? But now he's just the go-between, the real work is done by armed soldiers. It's been going on for over a year now but it's only in the last few months that I've made a point of watching it . . . Edwin's secret post-office."

She let go of his hand, shifting in his arms, drawing her knees up. What he had thought was a birthmark at the base of her spine now appeared to be a fading welt—from a riding crop?

"It goes in both directions," she went on. "The British use tinkers to send packets to Edwin, and Edwin replies with his escort of soldiers. But it all goes through Mad Jack Drum. Sometimes it's not just letters. Sometimes it's money."

"And the soldiers?"

She stretched an arm to the end of the bunk, revealing another faint scar. "They're from a local regiment encamped in the hills supposedly to protect the city in case of mutiny. In fact, they're in place to serve Edwin."

"And the commander is a tall man, broad shoulders, pocked face? Goes by the name of Tarr?"

"I think so. Yes."

"What about the British end?"

"It's somewhere up the Hudson along that same stretch as the White Swan. But Clinton won't dirty his hands with it, so he sends an adjunct."

"John André . . . ?" Said more to himself than to her.

She slid into his arms again, head on his shoulder, "Now, it's only through Mad Jack that I know about any of this. Edwin's never mentioned it, but Jack sometimes mistakes me for a daughter that he lost to the pox, and he likes to talk."

"What are the signals they use?"

"A triangle at the crossroads. Lanterns in a window at night."

"How is Tarr alerted when a packet's ready for delivery?"

She smiled. "They put a twist of the best tobacco in the dray that supplies the encampment."

"Who does it?"

"I don't know. Jack, I suppose." Then suddenly lifting her head as if startled, "You won't hurt him, will you? Jack's just an old fool who loves his ale and worships the Brotherhood. He thinks he's doing it all for General Washington. I don't care what you do to the others, but don't let them hurt Jack."

Laying her back down, she shut her eyes again and began to toy with his hair.

"Why didn't you tell me all this before? Why did you wait until now?"

Her lips pressed his. "Because I had to be certain."

"About what?"

Another kiss like a breath of wind. "About you."

It was still raining when they parted on the docks, a thin rain, hardly more than a mist. Her face was unusually pale against the dark folds of her cloak. Her hand was not quite steady on his arm.

"When will I see you again?"

He drew her closer, pressing her head to his chest. "I don't know." He felt her trembling slightly. The worse, he supposed, was yet to come—the longing like a blade in the gut.

"I have to tell you," she said suddenly. "Yes, I have to tell you."

Her face against his chest, his hand cradling her head.

"About that White Swan killer. I think he's still alive."

He traced the outline of a bruise with his finger. "Edwin told you?"

"It wasn't so much what he said, but the look in his eyes, the tone of his voice. Trust me, my instincts. I've had to trust them all my life to stay alive. Dawes is still alive."

It was not quite dawn when Grove returned to the Dwarf. The scent of her perfume had not entirely faded. He worried that if he slept he might wake up to find he couldn't summon a memory of her face, but the exhaustion was finally more than he could bear.

chapter
twenty-eight

That so-called Parson's Rise was actually little more than a wooded knoll adjacent to the Jersey road. Jack Drum's cottage was mostly hidden by a cluster of maples, while past a millpond stood the darker oaks where Tallmadge had left the bulk of his command: two score light cavalry armed with saber and carbines.

Although several members of this escort had taken part in the affair at the Dog Marsh, by and large these men represented a different caliber of soldier than Grove had used so far. They were front-line veterans, tested at Germantown and the inferno at Monmouth, once country boys now with years of experience in the saddle. They had proved themselves to be a disciplined force even in the face of withering fire. So regardless of what they may have personally felt about Matty Grove, they were prepared as soldiers to follow him. Monk was also on hand, an incongruous figure in this setting.

It was four in the afternoon, the tenth day of September. In spite of British advances in North Carolina, American morale was high since the arrival of Rochambeau and six thousand French troops at Newport. Also reassuring was Benedict Arnold's assuming command of the key defense at West Point.

Such events of the larger picture were not in Grove's mind as he approached this Parson's Hill cottage with Tallmadge and Monk. He was concentrated on more personal things: memories of Nancy Claire in the half-light, a special invitation in her eyes and, as expected, the subsequent emptiness like a constant hunger. For Grove, she was not only to be the reward . . . she was the spark to ignite the powder behind the ball.

He continued up the path amid a beautiful setting, with butterfly weed in flower along the banks of the pond and clinging blossoms of the so-called love vine. As they neared the small stone cottage they heard the tinkle of a harp.

The cottage was a tidy place with a single room below and two smaller lofts above. The hearth was a massive rough stone. The table—little more than a wooden plank on a trestle—was waisthigh . . . it seemed Mad Jack Drum ate his meals standing up. There were no chairs, only stools and a bench where Jack now sat with his harp.

He was a gray stick of a man with gaunt features and deep-set eyes. A mangy dog with a head that startingly resembled its master's lay by the hearth. There were many books along the walls, more stacked below the staircase. Most were poor editions in cowskin, but some were printed on good paper with copper cuts. Grove assumed they came from Hyde.

The old man hardly reacted when Grove and Monk and Tallmadge entered. His eyes were shut, his left cheek pressed against the frame of the harp, fingers still plucking out a tune called "The

Oppression of the Hills." At last taking note of the uniforms: "Now don't tell me that Mr. Washington has sent you boys as well?"

Grove nodded. "I'm afraid he did just that, Jack."

"Well, then you might as well pour yourself a bit from that jug because he'll never forgive me if you don't." The ale was local brew and there were only two cups. "And I don't suppose it's a packet of letters you've come for because I don't have it. Not today." He reached into the pocket of his shabby green coat and took out a small leather pouch. "Today this stuff is for smoking, not for calling Mr. Tarr."

Grove left his stool and took the pouch from Drum's hand. It was not the same blend that had been sent up the road the previous day, but it was close.

"From what direction does he come, Jack? From the north?"

Drum shook his head with a dazed grin. "Now, what am I to do with a lad who won't listen?"

Although seemingly engrossed with his harp again and a tune called "The Parting Cup," he noticed when Monk took a book from the shelf. "And what have we here? Another student of the practical sciences? Or is it the distant philosophies that you want? If so, he's come to the right place, because that's my specialty, yes it is. Did I happen to ask you gentlemen whether or not you were acquainted with the three great mysteries?"

"What mysteries would those be, Jack?"

"Why, the plumb line, compass, and level."

"No trowel?"

A glance to the window, a momentary frown. "Well, that's another matter, isn't it?"

Drum's eyes gradually closed. "Did you gents know there's a lodge in Concord that don't want any arms at all? Not even a wee knife the size of your thumb. It comes down from the Ancients, I hear, who also kept no arms but could go safe through enemy countries on account of their holiness. In the army they carried a flag of truce, and, like the books says over there, neither was a naked sword to be held in their presence." He seemed pleased with his recital.

"But weapons come in all shapes and sizes these days, don't they, Jack? If one were to take that trowel, for example, and give it a cutting edge . . ."

A frown. "Now doesn't that just show what you know, sir? That's not a weapon, it's a symbol."

"A symbol, Jack?"

"Sure. To inspire the good Brethren to unity . . . nothing can be fitted together without the trowel, which connects the stones by the proper arrangement of cement."

"What if one of those stones should crack, Jack?"

Silence, the man's eyes filling with tears. Mad Jack knew enough to know his loss. "You wouldn't by chance go by the name of Mr. Matty Grove, would you? The fella who stuck a knife in the ribs of more poor fools than a man can count on his hand?"

"It could be, Jack."

"And you wouldn't by chance have laid a little twist of tobacco in the back of a cart to lure Nathan Tarr to my house?"

"Yes, Jack." And Grove marveled at how at once removed and shrewd the man could be.

"Well, now, didn't I tell them something like this was bound to happen sooner or later?" Then nudging the still sleeping hound with his foot, "Come on, you damn fool, stand up. You happen to be in the presence of a famous man who just might put a noose around me neck, so stand up and give him a wag of your tail."

After these exertions not-so-mad Mad Jack stayed quiet, his hands continuing to play on the strings of the harp. Even after a lieutenant had entered to announce that Mr. Tarr and a body of horsemen were approaching, Drum appeared once more removed from it all.

Grove and Tallmadge went back to the oaks above the mill-pond, from which they had a fairly unobstructed view of the road and adjacent pasture but only to the ends of the dale. Such a field should have favored the aggressor, being narrow and affording little cover. Mounted soldiers attacked from the flank would find themselves corralled. Which was precisely what now concerned Tallmadge—unless Tarr immediately surrendered, he believed, the man's only option would be to fight to the death.

For opposite reasons Grove was against the alternative proposal that would have allowed Tarr to approach the cottage before any attempt was made to take him. Once Tarr got to the rise, Grove said, the field became too open. And would Tarr dismount or stay on the path with the main body of his escort and wait for old Jack to appear? "We should remember," Grove said, "that regardless of everything else, he's still a capable officer—"

"Also, I hope, a reasonable one," Tallmadge said. "Otherwise this is going to be a very grim day."

Tallmadge now raised an arm above his head, slowly brought it down. Moments later a portion of his party began to disperse along the line of foliage that bordered the path to the cottage. The rest stayed in the circle of oaks but prepared their horses. Weapons were primed—fusils and French carbines. The loads were the buck and ball that had devestated the British at Concord.

Grove and Tallmadge descended to the clearing and mounted their horses. In addition to pistols, both men now carried swords—Grove's a plain weapon with a sharkskin grip and rounded pommel, Tallmadge's an ornate piece with a silver hilt and ivory grip.

"Would you consider having one of my boys approach Tarr in your place?" Tallmadge said. "As a precaution?"

Grove, still priming his weapon, did not respond at first, then said, "I owe the man at least a word."

"Then shout it from a distance, or put it on paper. Because I would guess his word will be very disagreeable."

Grove added, "And tell your men to aim low, for the horses. It'll give Tarr's people half a chance—"

"For what?" Tallmadge leaned forward in the saddle. "You were never close to the man, were you?"

"We had some times. And he's still wearing our uniform. You don't ignore that."

At which point there was a low whistle from the bluff, followed by a soft reply from below. In response, Tallmadge signaled with his saber, extending the blade.

There were eighteen in Nathan Tarr's escort, armed with carbines and horse pistols. They came as a fine column, skirting the edge of the millpond and reminding Grove of days in White Plains when Tarr had led small parties into combat to the tune of "The White Cockade." Then as now he sat stiff in the saddle on account of a wound he had received at Quebec. As he came closer, Grove noted that Tarr still carried a favorite sidearm— a modified blunderbuss with a load known to drop both horse and rider at a hundred paces.

Grove waited until Tarr's men had drawn into the line of fire before coming forward and riding out at an easy pace, his hands plainly visible. His pistols, too, so that only the dagger in the sleeve of his right arm stayed hidden. At the center of the path he reigned in but did not dismount. As Tarr and his party came closer, Grove lifted an arm in a half-salute, Tarr replied with a nod. They faced one another from six paces: Tarr flanked by two junior officers, Grove still keeping his hands in plain sight. Although several of Tarr's party had withdrawn weapons, all was quiet except for the breath and shifting hooves of restless mounts.

"So, Matty, what little bird has put you in my path today?"

209

Cocking firelocks, ramrods in barrels.

"No bird, Nate, just a twist of Virginia's tobacco."

Tarr's jaws stayed taut. "So that's the game . . . you've deceived an old friend, and now expect to arrest him."

"I'm not alone, Nate. Ben Tallmadge's in those trees, with more than forty."

Tarr glanced back to the oaks, then over his shoulder to the waiting column—counting guns, noting the distance, marking the condition of the field. "I don't suppose you'd take a little advice from an old soldier, would you?"

Grove waited.

"Ride on, Matty. Take Ben and his men and ride on. Because I can't let you take me, not for all the gold in a certain gentleman's purse."

Sounds of withdrawing sabers, bayonets fitting to the muzzles.

"Nate, at least consider your men—"

"Ah, well now, that would seem to be your problem, wouldn't it? Because far be it from them to let loose the first shot."

Yet even as he spoke, Tarr's fingers had already closed on that blunderbuss, the muzzle nearly clear of the saddle. And in response Grove had let his right arm drop so that the dagger slid into his palm, wrist cocked at his thigh . . .

Tarr brought his weapon level with Grove's chest and slowly . . . very slowly . . . began squeezing the trigger. Grove understood that Tarr was probably less set on killing than on dying, but he still couldn't keep his dagger from releasing . . . end over end in a brief flash of light into Nathan Tarr's chest.

Then it seemed everyone was shouting at once, although it wasn't until Tarr's weapon slipped from his hands and discharged that a volley broke from the trees—a single shot, then another, and then several in succession.

The horses took the worst of it, some thrashing on the path, others bolting with wounds in the legs and rumps. A young soldier . . . a boy . . . with a smashed foot had begun to scream.

210

Two others lay pinned beneath their mares. Tarr, having slipped from the saddle and collapsed to the grass, called for quarter, but at least four more animals fell with their riders before Tallmadge ordered the cease-fire.

Blood and death had taken the day.

chapter
twenty-nine

The wounded were brought to the White Hill cottage to be attended by a regimental surgeon named Roger Holland. Seven needed his care: five with wounds in the limbs, two in more serious condition. Another had been killed outright. And there was Tarr . . .

While his men were attended to below Tarr was in an upstairs chamber with a quantity of rum and a bandage on his wound. It was now about nine in the evening, light provided by two burning splints. When Grove entered the room he thought Tarr was asleep, until suddenly the eyes opened.

"Would you like to see what you've done to me?" Tarr said.

"Would you like to take a look at this hole in my chest?" His voice was like something heard under water.

"Want to talk about it?"

Tarr laughed, coughed. "Talk about what? How you cut down my lads and stuck that blade of yours through my lungs? We were supposed to have been in the same damn army. Anyway, I'm dying."

"It was never your neck I was after, Nathan. It's Edwin Hyde's I want."

"Then talk to him, because I've got nothing to say to the bastard who's killed me."

"Tell me something, Nate, if you're so strong behind Mr. Hyde, then why did you give me the name of Dawes' whore? Seems you've been playing both ends against the middle."

Tarr had risen to an elbow—a painful movement that started him bleeding again. "I'm not like you, Matty. I've got a wife and a boy who's nearly come of age I can die on them but I can't leave without giving them something."

"And you believe Hyde will provide for them?"

"Not Hyde, others."

"What others?"

"Do I really need to spell it out for you?"

"The Order."

"It's more than that, more than you can imagine . . ."

"Tell me something else, Nate. Whatever became of that Mr. Tarr I knew at White Plains? What in hell became of him?"

"How should I know? Maybe he died of mistaken glory and a little dose of greed."

"Is that what you'll want on your stone? *Mistaken glory and a little dose of greed?*"

"It's better than some I've seen. Anyway, my reputation will hardly be of concern to the worms."

He shut his eyes then. "Let me die, Matty . . . let me die now."

"Nate, tell me what Hyde is trying to do—"

"Too late." But as Grove moved to the door: "Matty, wait. Is it true you have a letter from Clinton's office that was stolen by those two murdered spies of yours?"

"Yes."

"And you hven't been able to make sense of it even with the help of that Mr. Monk?"

"That's right. Look, Nate, I don't want you to—"

"Then what you want is in my saddlebag. Give it to Monk. He'll know what to do with it . . . go on, get it, and give it to Monk. And then, damn you, don't come back here."

Tarr died shortly after midnight, but it was not until dawn that Grove learned of his death. By this time two wagons had arrived to transport the wounded, and a meal had been prepared for those with the stomach for it. It was a beautiful morning with the first signs of turning leaves.

In addition to the wounded it had been decided that Jack Drum should be removed, and Grove was watching from the meadow when the old man was led away, moving off in a ragged tunic from the Colonial wars, the harp in his arms, the dog at his heels. Next the bodies were removed: junior officers in canvas, Tarr in a plain coffin. As the procession continued along the path Tallmadge approached Grove from behind.

Without waiting for Grove to turn and face him he said, "I think His Excellency will want to know—"

"Know what?"

"About Tarr . . . Why do you suppose he did it—drew that blunderbuss of his and then hesitated? He must have known the consequences—"

"Then the man was a soldier."

"Yes, but that doesn't explain why he apparently wanted to die."

"He preferred it to living in disgrace."

"That's nice, but not enough of an answer for the general."

"Then wait until Monk has finished with what he found in Tarr's saddlebag."

chapter
thirty

What was in Nathan Tarr's saddlebag was a book, a volume of some three hundred pages originally published in 1775 under the title *The Spirit of Masonry*. The author was a Mr. William Hutchinson—solicitor, antiquarian, novelist and eventual Master of the Masonic Lodge at Barnard Castle in England. Intended to serve as a kind of handbook for novitiates, the work consisted of lectures on the institutions, rites and ceremonies of the Lodge. But it was not the contents of this book that was of interest ... it was the sequence of its pages, the arrangement of words on those pages. Which was to say the book was only of interest for yielding up the key to understanding the letter extracted from Mr. Clock's wooden leg.

It was now about two in the afternoon. The book appeared to be a kind of dictionary . . . that was how Arthur Monk described it after some three hours. By this time the Parson's Rise was deserted except for six members of Tallmadge's party who had been charged with securing the grounds. The cottage had been tidied, the linen burned, the worst of the blood scrubbed from the floorboards.

Monk worked in the room where Tarr had died, and it was here that Tallmadge and Grove now came to discuss the Clock letter.

Monk began. "Do you remember," he said to Grove, "that when you first brought me this document I told you that a complete understanding would be impossible without the key-text the cipher depends on? Well, it seems we have the key-text."

He cleared off a small table, leaving only Mr. Hutchinson's book and a facsimile of the Clock letter. Tallmadge settled on the bed where Tarr had died the night before. Grove took the stool by the window. Monk had already spent enough time in this room to leave his imprint: papers spread across every available surface, pastry crumbs and bits of cheese along the windowsill. There were also several volumes from Jack Drum's collection strewn about the floor, and at least one more curious sketch of that blazing eye on top of a pyramid.

"We should start with the premise," Monk began. "A figure of standing in our ranks has become dissatisfied with the course of this revolution. We'll call him Edwin. He distrusts Washington, particularly insofar as His Excellency is worshiped by that very same mob that Edwin finds distasteful. What is Edwin to do? He's not a Tory. He's even a Whig of some importance. So while he doesn't want to submit to England, he also fears and dislikes this Revolution. But Edwin isn't alone. To organize these gentlemen Edwin finds it convenient to go *beyond* the issues. He turns to the Order . . . or at least the part of the Order he sees eye to eye with. His recruitment of these gentlemen is a gradual

217

process, and many—maybe all—will never be told the whole truth. After all, these men aren't traitors. But here's a foundation Edwin can build his trust on. These men are internationalists. Despite hostilities they've continued to maintain ties with the British, and they would hate to give up their standing and their position to some back-alley beggar in a uniform."

Monk turned to another sheaf of notes, and Tallmadge took out a flask of brandy. Grove stayed at the window.

"It's possible," Monk went on, "that the British were first approached as early as, say, '77. But I don't think they would have been too receptive until after Saratoga and the French commitment. Then it appears that Edwin met a warm reception. And why not? After all, he was approaching them as a friend and equal. And he wasn't just dealing with military officers or the king's ministers. Mostly it was with men like himself who had never particularly believed in this war and resented the cost.

"What did he say to them? I imagine he would have told them what they already knew: that this war was hopeless for England in the long run. Next, and I think this must have made an impression, he would have told them that if this conflict didn't end amicably, Britain would lose the right of trade and investment. And then came the solution: 'Hand me this nation and I shall insure that you enjoy a piece of the prosperity.' 'Very well,' they might have replied, 'but how are we supposed to hand you the nation?'

"To which Edwin would have answered: 'Oh, I'll arrange *that* when the time is right.' He would be careful not to tell too much, or more than he knew but couldn't admit to not knowing."

A quick glance to Grove. "At any rate, that's the premise. But I think it's safe to say that Edwin's plans are by now well-advanced. His confederates are in key positions and I think it's not unlikely he has the tacit agreement of at least one general of standing. All this must have required a great deal of correspondence, which is what Smith and Dearborn witnessed . . . and essentially why they were murdered."

Another brief pause as Monk discarded his notes and picked up that facsimile of the original sixteen blood-spattered pages. "About the format," Monk said. "Although the work bears Clinton's stamp as British commander for the Americas, I suspect the author was his adjutant John André. He's couched the thing in terms of a business proposition. There's a fair bit I still have to work out but I think the gist should be clear. So unless you have any specific questions . . ."

Lifting the page at an awkward angle because he had mislaid his spectacles, he began to read: " 'Dear Ancient and Honorable Sirs, permit me to present the following intelligence with my deepest regards and respect for your office.' There's a marginal note here that seems to indicate the letter was jointly addressed to William Eden as His Majesty's director of intelligence, Lord North and four others who I imagine represent the economic side of things. Yet in that they all appear to maintain an allegiance with the Order, André simply addresses them: 'Let me additionally offer, My Dear Brethren, our humblest respect to the Society, its Laws, Charges and Occupations.' There's then a short explanation of content to indicate that what is about to be read is a report on activities and agreements of a third body. Which is to say that André is merely the go-between. 'Let it further be known that all forthwith intelligence has been offered in good faith by our American Brethren with the Authority of their Lodge and Master.' From this point forward, however, this Master is referred to as Hiram, which appears to be a name Edwin has used before.

"It then goes on thus: 'In accordance with earlier agreements, Hiram has informed me that he is at last prepared to take a bold and effective step to rid us of our enemies, seize their floundering ship, and end this needless conflict. He is to accomplish this with the aid of various confederates, some of whom are known to you as worthy Brethren. Others shall be known only when the thing is done.'

"It goes on more specifically: 'On or about a date to be approved by circumstances, Hiram agrees to furnish us with the following. In the first place he will dispose of those whom we fear most and have consistently caused us grief. In the second place he will provide us with the means to deal our common enemies an effective and demoralizing blow. In the third place he will establish himself as the Master of this house through the good and respected names of his confederates. In the fourth place he will arrange a peace with us that will assure our profit upon this vast and bountiful land.'

"There's a last bit, as I say, that I haven't worked out, but I think it deals with resources in the army. It goes like this: 'Hiram would further assure us that at least one of his confederates has proven himself to be a'—and I believe the next word is *capable*, but may be *popular*—'commander of the military, and thus awaits only the opportunity to assume his rightful command. Thereupon he will speedily curtail any social discord and unrest as may accompany this transition of power while also maintaining a firm hand upon the Capitol.' Next there's a reference to a mutiny, which may figure in the plan as we discussed earlier, which is to say they intend to use the excuse of a mutiny to invoke dictatorial powers. Finally there's a list of names: Abraxas, Pythagoras, Philo, Aristobulus.

"It goes on in a little different fashion. 'In accordance with earlier agreements, Hiram would have me affirm the following: Upon the establishment of his Authority and that of his partners he will present us with a fair and equitable share in tobacco, hemp, salt, indigo . . .' and four other words here that I can't make out . . . 'in turn the Management of these Concerns shall reside with him and his partners. Nor shall there be tolerated any further imposition of a foreign will except as previously stipulated in correspondence.'

"The last bit uses another device, apparently relying on a Masonic foundation. I'd guess this was André's personal choice and that he's enjoying the drama here. It goes like this: 'Although our Brother wishes no offense, he would have me remind you that his reach is not limited to this land. And as the Ancients sought out and took vengeance on those who betrayed his namesake, so too is he prepared to take vengeance on those who would betray him. He would further have me remind you that Authority is not a subject for the meek or faint of heart and that this must be kept in mind if and when his Demogorgon—also known to you as Caliban—is called on to collect a debt. Know also that although his method is terrible, his cause is Right and exact with the skill of the rectangle, the weight and plumb line. It is the Trowel, however, that he favors. The Trowel works to seal the Temple by removing the unclean flesh.' There's then something about moneylenders, another reference to the French, I suspect. And there's some sort of incantation I still can't make sense of."

After a lengthy, awkward silence, Tallmadge felt obliged to ask Monk to leave the room.

"I owe you an apology," Tallmadge said when Monk left. "I doubted your judgment—"

Grove shook his head. "It's not necessary."

"I'd like to hear your evaluation of all this. How do you see it?"

"I think Monk summed it up pretty damn well. Dissatisfied with this revolution, Hyde is about to seize the reins of this government and steer a new course . . . something more profitable for himself and his confederates."

"And this is to be achieved by the betrayal of various strategies."

221

"Yes."

"And what about those confederates? What do you make of them?"

"I think they're pawns in all this, unwitting pawns of no real consequence without Hyde. On the other hand, I doubt they'll fail to play out Edwin's game if various positions in this government were offered on a silver platter. After all, they see eye-to-eye with Hyde in most areas, and so no doubt are against the direction of this war."

"And who would you include in their ranks? Arnold?"

"Maybe."

"Morris? Tom Paine? I'm trying to get to the extent of this thing."

"All right. It seems Edwin Hyde is about to steal this government in collaboration with the British. Is that plain enough?"

"Aye, it's plain."

"We don't, however, know exactly how he plans to do it . . . and until we find out he's got the advantage."

"Yes, he still has the advantage . . ." He moved to Grove's side at the window. "What are you thinking, Matty? Right now, tell me your thoughts."

Not facing him, "I think it would be a good thing if Edwin Hyde had an accident. On the road, for example."

Tallmadge moved away from the window. "I thought so. But I can't believe I'll ever get approval for that—"

"Then don't ask for approval. Just say—'Rid me of Hyde.' Just *say* it."

"I can't."

"Can't you look the other way?"

"No, not without first talkng to His Excellency—"

"And when will you do that?"

"Not sure, but I'll be leaving for the Hudson tonight."

"And meanwhile?"

"Hold your fire."

The rain had subsided. Monk wandered out across the meadow, leaving a trail of bootprints in the grass. The half dozen dragoons from Tallmadge's escort were still below—getting drunk.

"By the way," Tallmadge said as he and Grove descended the staircase, "Is that reference to Caliban and Demogorgon a reference to Dawes?"

"Probably."

"Well, at least that's one problem we needn't worry about . . . correct?"

Grove stopped midstride. "Say what's on your mind, Benjamin."

"Well, there have been rumors that Dawes is still alive, that he managed to make it across the river that night."

"And what are these rumors supposed to be based on?"

"I don't know . . . something about slaughtered livestock to the north . . ."

"And you believe it?" Grove certainly did. Had suspected it all along.

Tallmadge continued moving down the staircase, faster than before. "I would also keep an eye on Miss Nancy Claire. I think we'll need her, after all."

After leaving Tallmadge on the high road, Grove and Monk proceeded south at a strong pace but still had no hope of reaching the city before midnight. With the earlier downpour the road was not firm, and their mounts had not been sufficiently rested or fed.

Thoroughly frightened, Monk spent the first part of the journey trying to engage Grove in conversation . . . Was it smart to leave the Rise unattended? . . . What about the consequences of Nathan Tarr's death? . . . Did Grove have any thoughts about how Washington might respond? . . . What about the eventual outcry from Congress? . . . Did he think Nancy Claire knew—? Grove exploded then and told Monk to shut his mouth.

From then on there was nothing to keep Monk from recalling every sort of tale about ghosts that haunted the neighboring glens and thieves that prowled the broad fields. Now and again he even found himself glancing back over his shoulder with a vague sense of someone behind them. Some sort of murderous ghoul . . . Foolish, crazy thoughts for a man of science, he instructed himself. But he was only half-listening.

chapter
thirty-one

In her narrow trundle bed, young Sarah was also afflicted with fears this night. Nameless fears built out of unpleasant stories heard throughout the neighborhood, fragments of rumors in the market stalls. They were like a sickness. She felt tired but not able to sleep, hungry but not able to eat, too warm and too cold.

It had begun that morning when on her uncle's instructions she had gone to a chandler's shop to buy a ready-dressed ham, a half-quarter loaf and some bran, and heard two servants from nearby establishments talking about what had supposedly happened at Parson's Rise—the execution of several Pennsylvania Riflemen by order of Matty Grove. They said the order had been given in order to stop a local mutiny, but questions had been

225

raised about what evidence Grove had acted on. After all, it was only a few weeks earlier that the man had nearly killed two boys in Cutter's Lane just because he hadn't liked the look of them ... And not more than a block away from the chandler's shop there was talk about the discovery three nights earlier of a mutilated lamb along the road to Germantown. Of course a slaughtered animal was nothing to raise eyebrows but the creature had been left in a by now too familiar state—the intestines laid to the shoulder, the tongue and hoof cut away. It had not been eaten, so one had to conclude the beast had been killed for ugly sport.

"Well, what does your bold Matty Grove have to say about *that?*" Sarah was asked by at least three meddlesome parties. "What does he have to say about this poor butchered beast after telling the world he'd rid us of the monster?"

"He needn't say anything at all," Sarah had told them, "because it's all a pack of lies." She fought back tears as she said it.

By midmorning there were more details suggesting the story had at least some basis in fact. It was said the creature had been discovered by a pig-jobber who fainted straight away at the sight of it. The animal had been laid dead center at the crossroads so the entire country would know the White Swan killer was back for business.

As the day wore on there were additional details about what had happened at Parson's Rise, and the conclusion was that Mr. Grove had at last bit off more than he could chew. Sarah also noted several strange officers about, congressmen with serious faces and brooding dragoons. When she was preparing a meal for a late-rising guest, and broke an egg into a pan only to discover that the yolk bore a bloodstain, well, it was too much.

For some time after retiring to her bedroom Sarah did her best to keep her mind on other things: the prospect of Tuesday and rice pudding, Christmas and the Governor's Ball. She thought, dreamed as did many others her age, about traveling west, where it was said the land was filled with all sorts of wonderous sights such as great prairies where buffalo grew to the size of schooners and any seed dropped in soil would sprout overnight and a race of ancient wizards lived in caves of red cliffs and streams rang like chimes with the tinkle of gold against the pebbles and pines were as tall as the tallest steeples and there was a canyon the size of an ocean. Not to mention a forest that had turned to stone, and a place where the sky was almost always blue even in the depths of winter.

For a while, diverted by these thoughts, she was even able to doze. Then, perhaps prompted by the wind and banging shutters, her mind returned to Grove. She had never understood the man, but in spite of her age there were moments when she felt she could sense his moods—whether he was frustrated or concerned, angry or exhausted.

On this night, after distinguishing his footsteps on the staircase, she judged, imagined, that he was frightened—for the first time since he had been here.

She thought of going to him, knocking gently on his door to ask if there was not something else he wished . . . a slice of pie, perhaps, a portion of the ham from the chandler's shop, a pint of something to help him sleep . . . ?

But as she reached for her gown she heard a woman's voice calling to Grove from the yard below. Then the sound of a dropping latch, and footsteps on the staircase again.

She waited until the footsteps had faded before slipping out of bed and tiptoeing to a window above the yard. Her view was somewhat restricted by the branches of an elm, but it was clear enough that the woman had come to deliver some message, the subject of which had made her hysterical.

At first Sarah supposed the message concerned the White Swan killer. Had the monster been spotted? Had he committed another murder? But as Grove hurried off to fetch his cloak the messenger moved out from the shadows and became recognizable as the maid employed by Miss Nancy Claire.

Sarah could not claim to know the servant well, but they had seen one another often enough in the streets and on occasion, as shoppers did, had even exchanged a word or two. She was was African or Indian and it was said that she practiced some form of witchcraft, which partially accounted for the beauty of her mistress. Clearly, though, there was no magic at work tonight.

Sarah stayed at the window for some time after Grove and Miss Claire's servant had departed—gazing into the empty yard, listening to the echo of pounding hooves and the rattle of a carriage. In the wake of this clamor were the cries of dogs. She could also imagine the ugly whispers of mean folks speculating on what new crises Matty Grove had brought down on this city.

At last returning to her bed, she lay down in the darkness and gave way to the tears she had been holding back for so many hours.

chapter
thirty-two

Miss Claire was also alone in darkness relieved only by a candle burnt low in the socket that her eyes remained fixed on. She wore a simple gown, a length of silk thrown over the shoulders. What might have been a pattern of rose petals were in fact flecks of blood, though this was not immediately obvious. She lay on her stomach, chin on her arm. The french doors to the garden were ajar, revealing a broken pane of glass. The mirror had been shattered, fragments of porcelain littered the rug.

When Grove came into the room she said nothing, did not even stir. Then at last without looking at him . . . "Go away, Matty. There's nothing you can do for me now."

As his eyes became accustomed to the darkness he could make

out additional clues to what had happened—bruises on her wrist, the handle of a riding crop showing from beneath the counterpane.

He moved closer but her face was still hidden. "Why did you send for me if—"

"I didn't send for you. It was Nina's idea . . . and a poor one at that."

The maid, who until now had been watching from the doorway, withdrew down the corridor.

"I'm not angry with her. After all, I too once believed that Mr. Matty Grove was capable of protecting me . . . a mistake."

He moved still closer, knelt beside her on the floor. "Why don't you just tell me what happened . . . ?"

A slight tremor in her shoulders, but her voice was still flat. "What do you *think* happened?"

He picked up a length of leather binding, used to secure her wrists to the bedpost. Her ankles, however, must have been tied with strips of material from her garments.

"He couldn't have know that you had anything to do with what happened at Parson's Rise . . ."

"Unlike you, Mr. Grove, Edwin doesn't need proof to act. Suspicion is all he requires. Anyway I admitted it . . ."

"*Why?*"

She propped herself up on her elbows, her gown sliding past her shoulder and revealing welts—parallel wounds suggesting methodical work. "In order to get him to *stop*, Mr. Grove."

He reached for her hand. "Nancy, look at me."

"Go *away*, Matty. They're right what they say about you. People die around you. At least I'm still alive—"

He got to his feet and went to the table. Her tiny pistol lay amid the remnants of several torn cartridges. Apparently she'd tried to load the thing before collapsing on the bed.

"Do you know why he didn't kill me?" she said suddenly. "Even after I'd betrayed him . . . do you know why?" She gave him no chance to answer. "Because he doesn't consider me a threat. Not any longer. He knows I've told you what I know. What more damage can I do? And I think it's more than that . . . it's so typical of him . . . he's leaving you a message, a challenge. What are you going to do about it? he's saying. He's that sure of himself, and it looks like he's right . . ."

Grove wouldn't tell her what he now knew . . . the less she knew from here on the less danger she would be in, but he did need to give her some hope . . . "I want you to know I talked to Tallmadge and—"

"Ben Tallmadge? And what will *he* do?"

"It's what he thinks you can do. If you gave testimony against Hyde—"

"And Congress would take my word over his? He'd laugh in our faces."

She drew her gown to her shoulder. "And there's another reason Edwin let me live. He knows that I know there's no place to hide from him. Even if we were to go off, sooner or later he'd find us . . . You don't believe me, do you? Well, I've seen him do it before. He'll stop at nothing to take his pound of flesh . . . even if we got to China, even then he'd track us down."

Looking away, he noticed the ebony dagger lying in the fragments of glass. It was hardly an equalizer.

"Matty . . ." Her tone had changed. Stronger, and seductive too. "Matty, there's really only one solution now. Sooner or later he'll see that the job is finished. There won't be any life for me . . . or us. Matty, you've got to kill him . . ."

He agreed, and for reasons that went beyond the two of them. But he also remembered Tallmadge's warning to wait . . . He saw the handle of the riding crop again, knew what it had done. As he moved to the door he said, "Where is he?"

She hesitated.

"Where?"

"I'm not sure. Perhaps the Hudson . . ."

The Traitor

"What's his business there?"

"I don't know. He may have gone to meet someone—"

"Who?"

She glanced at his hands, his boots, his pistol. "It's just a guess, Matty . . ."

"Who?"

"The White Swan killer."

Given the hour and weather—dawn in the grip of a premature frost—only a handful of citizens could claim to have seen Matty Grove's departure from the city. Young Sarah was among them, but she had little to say.

After collecting his belongings and settling his account he left as he'd come: moving at an unhurried pace through the back lanes, ignoring the gaze of those who watched from cracks in the shutters. He did, in fact, say goodbye, and even briefly took her hand. But this was not something she would ever be willing to share with the others.

The
High Ground

chapter
thirty-three

It was not until the last week of September that word of Grove and events in the north reached Philadelphia, and then it was the questionable word of a peddler named Archibald Nash. Mr. Nash may well have been a common figure on the roads and byways below the Hudson, but he was not one to be trusted— not with his shoddy displays of poor lace, inferior nails and useless tonics. The man was also not above dealing with Tories and the like assuming they were foolish enough to meet his price. Still, since he was the first to bring the news, remarkable news, folks had no alternative but to listen . . .

One blustery evening somewhere north of the Scotch Plains, Nash took shelter in an inn called the Blooming Sally, which had become a soldier's haunt, lying as it did in the cockpit of the war. Both Washington and Cornwallis had briefly stopped here at one time or another, so they said. Also a table had once been set for Sir Henry Clinton, who didn't care for the pie. On bleak nights, like the present one, the pipes of the slaughtered Black Watch could sometimes be heard calling from over the hills. There were also stories of a drummer boy seen passing through fields without disturbing a blade of grass as he walked in time to the death march.

Given such associations, Nash wasn't really surprised to enter the Sally and see Matty Grove seated before a joint of mutton, a mess of peas and a glass of pale ale. Actually it wasn't until he caught a glimpse of the dagger that Nash knew here was *the* Matty Grove, and even then he didn't let on. "I hope you don't mind if I join you at this table, sir."

"Not at all," said Grove.

"What direction are you headed?" Nash asked casually, and just as casually Grove indicated north.

"May I ask why?" Nash said.

"I'm hoping to find me some trouble," Grove said, trying to smile.

"Well," Nash told him, "then you're going to the right place. If the weather won't get you the Tories will. And if the Tories don't then the Redcoats will."

"And what do you know about the Redcoats?"

"Only what I've heard on the road."

"And what would that be?"

"Well, this may amaze you, Mr. Grove, but it's got to do with the capture of a British spy by the name of John Anderson. Those with a nose for such things say this Mr. Anderson wasn't just any old spy. He was an officer and gentleman attached directly to Henry Clinton's staff. And his real name isn't John Anderson. It's John *Andrew* . . . or at least something that sounded like Andrew but with more of a French ring to it."

"Could that name have been John André?" Grove asked.

"Well, now that you mention it, it could very well be the name I heard."

"And what is it that this Mr. John André was supposed to have done?"

"I don't rightly know. I only hear he was captured as he crossed a brook called Clark's Kill, which is more or less in Tarrytown, and that upon being searched incriminating papers were found concealed in his fine boot."

"Incriminating papers?"

"Yes, those papers incriminated one of Mr. Washington's most trusted generals—"

"And who might this general be?"

"It might be Mr. Benedict Arnold," said Nash, "the scourge of Quebec and commander of West Point . . . may his name forever be cursed . . ."

"So you're talking about treason . . ."

"Aye."

Grove suddenly forgot his supper, sat with hands knotted into fists. Then, as if speaking from some kind of trance, Grove asked where Benedict Arnold was at this moment.

"Fled," Nash replied. "Like a common thief. He's now with the Redcoats—"

"And André? Where is John André?"

"I hear Tappan, I hear Tarrytown. Whichever, it's known he's in the custody of Mr. Major Benjamin Tallmadge . . ."

"Where," Grove finally asked, "is Washington?"

"I'm only a simple peddler, not exactly privy to secrets of state."

Grove, annoyed at himself for his question, snapped that he understood that, but since Nash was so full of information he thought maybe he'd have this news of Washington too.

"Well," Nash told him, fully enjoying himself, "I'd say that regardless of where Mr. Washington is, he's bound to have his hands full—and not only on account of that Benedict Arnold but also on account of another strange matter—

"And *what* matter is that?"

"It's just this, Mr. Grove. As of last night His Excellency lost no less than two members of his personal escort, his Life Guards."

"What do you mean they were *lost?*"

"I *mean,* sir, that one moment they were doing whatever those Life Guards do and the next they were not to be found—vanished, it seems, right off the face of the earth. Now, of course, they may have only deserted, but given everything else it could be a whole lot worse—"

Grove was on his feet, calling for his horse.

Later Nash would tell about a corduroy road to a rickety bridge that in the best of weather was none too safe and in the midst of a storm highly dangerous. When Matty Grove came to the bridge, said Nash, he drove his horse into the air and sailed to the other side. Well, this was no more improbable than the combination of true events that Nash had just related.

chapter
thirty-four

Although it may well have been in Matty's mind to make for Tappan or so-called Orange Town, he actually crossed the Hudson above Haverstraw and did not stop until he stood opposite the cliffs at West Point. It was the morning of the twenty-sixth, and by now Nash's story had spread through the countryside and into the cities.

Grove and Tallmadge met just south of the grounds on the edge of a rocky knoll. From here they had a view of the landing where Arnold was supposed to have made his escape the previous Sunday. The far cliffs and garrison that he was to have handed to the British were also plainly in sight.

Having escorted the elegant Mr. André from North Salem,

239

Tallmadge had also spent a wretched night on the road. Nothing to eat except a lump of porridge, no opportunity to wash, except in the rain.

"I don't know what you've heard," Tallmadge said, "damn country's alive with rumors."

"Are they true?"

"Unfortunately many are."

Tallmadge turned to face the river and the imposing view of the opposite cliffs. There were several defensive systems at the Point, each protecting the other. They were supposed to be the key to the continent, impregnable . . . unless attacked overland from the west.

Tallmadge nodded toward the south. "André landed on Friday somewhere under Haverstraw. No flag. A surtout coat over his regimentals. Arnold met him ashore. They spoke until dawn—"

"And the terms?"

"Clinton to receive the Points. Arnold to receive a fixed sum and commission. When André returned, mostly by luck, he was captured at Tarrytown. His Excellency asked that I bring him here. Beyond that I know nothing."

"Why do they say Arnold did it?"

"Who's to know? Jealousy. Injured pride. I imagine he also hates the French, and the money must have counted for something. Still . . ."

"Where's his wife?"

"On her way to Philadelphia."

"And André?"

Tallmadge glanced back to the Robinson house, where all but one window remained shuttered.

"I'd like to talk to him."

"That wouldn't be wise, Matty."

"Why not?"

"His Excellency might well object—"

"Then let me speak with His Excellency."

"Impossible. The man's engaged at the Point. Anyway, he has enough on his hands at the moment. You must know that."

There were echoes of cannon, a single volley to test a battery that Arnold had purposely neglected. There were strains of fife and drum as the first defensive lines were deployed.

"I'll be frank with you," Tallmadge went on. "When this Arnold business broke I assumed the worst was over. Hyde had taken his best shot and failed. After all, your Clock letter more or less referred to just this sort of scheme. And one can't help but tend toward some optimism. Anyway, my first reaction was relief."

"And then you discovered the Life Guards?"

"What do you know of that?"

"Only that they've been posted missing, and that Hyde was recently in the valley."

"According to whom?"

"Let's call it an educated guess."

"Matty, if we hope to—"

"Nancy Claire, for some of it."

Tallmadge nodded, bit his lips. "Well, she told you the truth. Hyde is, was, in the area. Possibly to meet with Clinton, possibly to meet with Arnold. But I doubt that was the point of his visit. I think this whole Arnold business was only intended as a footnote to the larger plan. A minor footnote at that."

"And those guards?"

A second column marching to "A Toss of the Feathers" had by now descended from the battery at Sugarloaf.

"Sentries have been routinely posted since Sunday," Tallmadge said. "These two were near the wood down that road. The bodies were discovered by a local boy, who then told one of my lieutenants."

"Has the general been informed?"

"Yes."

241

The Traitor

"And no one saw or heard anything?"
"No."
"Where are the bodies now?"
"Forest hovel about a mile from here."
"May I see them?"
"I don't recommend it."

It was now ten o'clock, a slack hour for those involved in the Arnold affair. After dispersing riders on various missions, Washington spent much of the morning brooding over the loss of a friend and general who may well have been the best in either camp. He was also somewhat distraught over André's fate, and the fate of Arnold's wife, whom he had known for nearly eighteen years. On the cliffs riflemen continued to prepare for an expected British thrust, but all in all it was quiet, particularly along the lower eastern shore where Grove and Tallmadge now traveled.

There was a goat path leading from the shore, and it was here that the two dismounted before continuing into the wood. At first impression this place seemed idyllic with turning leaves and last blossoms of the season.

The cabin, or forest hovel as Tallmadge called it, might have belonged to any of the folks that inhabited these shores—a tinker, a woodcutter, a hermit. It was a single room structure with papered windows and a rough stone chimney. A sentry stood at the edge of the meadow. There were no other signs of life except a discarded bucket and an axe embedded in a stump.

Tallmadge kept to the path with a handkerchief pressed to his nose and mouth. The light inside was poor, and Grove hesitated in the door. The stench had attracted flies and beetles—hundreds of them that moved like rattling pebbles across the dirt-packed floor.

The bodies had been laid on a stout oak table and covered with a length of sailcloth. The boots seemed suspended in a rectangular shaft of dusty light that fell from a window opposite the door. Blood had drawn mice that fled as Grove advanced. Then, lifting the sailcloth, another swarm of flies.

Grove had heard the legend that if a man's last vision was that of his murderer, the image would forever be etched in his eyes. The eyes of these two would yield nothing. The first, a boy of about seventeen, appeared to have died suddenly. The wound at the throat was deep. The face suggested peace. The second, a man of about thirty, appeared to have struggled. A portion of the left ear was missing and there were ragged wounds about the neck and shoulders. The torsos and appendages were as expected, although the killer had not had time to remove the tongues.

When Grove came out of the hovel he found Tallmadge seated on a pine stump in a clearing amid the elms. His flask of brandy lay across one knee. "I'm open to any suggestions," he said.

"You might try burying them," Grove said. "But if you want an opinion I don't think this was premeditated. I'd say that Dawes wanted to take a look at us and those two got in his way."

"Then why did he . . . I mean, why would he—?"

"Because it's his nature. His training."

Tallmadge got to his feet, tried to compose himself. "What do you suggest?"

"When do you leave for Tappan?"

"Tomorrow, the next day."

"And the general?"

"Soon after."

"By what route?"

"Barge to Stony Point, then overland."

"How many to accompany him?"

"Twenty or so. What are you getting at?"

The Traitor

"That it would be wise if the general rode only with those he knows by name."

Tallmadge moved to the edge of the meadow and a broader view of the shore. There were trails of smoke from the Point— Benedict Arnold burning in effigy?

"So that's it," Tallmadge said. "You really believe they intend to murder His Excellency?"

"I think it's been part of the plan all along. What better way to insure Hyde's takeover—?"

"Then we'll double the guard."

"Dawes will smell a rat."

"Then what?"

"Proceed as usual and let me catch him when he surfaces—"

"It's a hell of a gamble, Matty."

"Well, if you send a party tramping down river he'll just disappear until another opportunity comes along. And there will be more bodies like the ones in there."

"And what about the Capital? I mean, we can no longer ignore the possibility that Hyde may be moving to seize the Capital right now as we speak."

"I'm glad you're coming around to my thinking about the man. But I don't think he'll commit himself until he knows that Washington is dead. Anyway, if you bring in a commander to defend the city you may end up with another traitor . . . the Brothers have a large and distinguished membership."

They led their mounts on foot to a narrow road off the path.

"I'm supposed to tell you that you're to take this only to the corporal's doorstep. No further."

Grove turned, looked at him. "What is this, that Freemason business again? His Excellency is afraid to move against Hyde out of fear of upsetting the Order?"

"It's not that. This is a delicate time, we've had endless disputes with the French about how to proceed in the south. And they—"

"Are Freemasons too? Dozens, I hear, are prominent Masons—"

"Whatever, the country can't stand a scandal just now—"

"Benjamin, Edwin Hyde has employed an assassin to murder your commander-in-chief. I'm betting he's also at least partly responsible for this Arnold affair. Now if *that* isn't scandal . . ."

"All the same it can still be claimed that Arnold acted alone, that his treason goes no further than himself."

"Whereas Hyde extends to the Order, and the Order extends everywhere?"

Tallmadge shrugged. "And you had also better stay clear of Nancy Claire. People may get the wrong idea about what your real motives are in all this."

Before Grove started down river again he and General Washington briefly exchanged glances from a distance of about one hundred yards. His Excellency, having embarked on another inspection of the West Point garrison, had been standing on the heights. Grove, having crossed to the western shore and changed horses, had been proceeding below and slightly to the south. The general lifted an arm in response to Grove's salute. Beyond this nothing passed between them, though Grove, noting Washington's exposure on the cliff, could not help envisioning a marksman with a Pennsylvania rifle concealed in the rocks.

chapter
thirty-five

It was about noon when Grove set out along this western shore, descending from the north. The landscape was as harsh as any Grove had encountered so far; the inhabitants a strange and unruly people. The White Swan Inn lay only about twenty miles to the south.

For the first leg of his journey Grove tried to put himself in Corporal Dawes' position, view this landscape in terms of how to kill a general named Washington en route from West Point. He kept his eye on the high ground . . . he could be hit by a bullet too. Now and then he consulted an inadequate map drawn the year before. And then he gave in to what had always been waiting to take over . . . he was only human after all . . . he found himself returning to Miss Nancy Claire, to their few hours together. At times he felt her alongside him, encouraging, urging him on. And it was with her voice in the wind that he now came on the cottage.

It was a small, quaint structure, like others he had passed by except that it stood above a particularly narrow passage of the river and there were no signs of life. None. According to his map this spot had no specific name but lay somewhere between the Point and Fort Montgomery. There had been recent Loyalist activity along the opposite shore, which added to his uneasiness.

He dismounted among a copse of elms, left his horse unfettered, proceeded up the steep rise. Although it was late in the day and getting chilly, there was no sign of a fire. Closer, he noted that the door had been left slightly ajar. When he saw the corpse of a dog in the yard he slipped into a tall cluster of alder bushes and withdrew his pistols.

From this vantage point the cottage and surrounding nook appeared inviting, with a peaked roof in well-laid thatch and sidings of split logs. A broad oak shaded a knoll about a thin brook, and a boxed garden of herbs suggested a woman's touch.

He tossed a handful of pebbles against the siding, waited until sure of no response, continued to advance. There were chestnuts below the knoll matted thick with wild-grape vines and clumps of timothy grass. Beyond lay a sandy hollow, and then a deer path to the brook. From the brook he could see through the window suspended strings of dried apples, ears of Indian corn and linsey-woolsey. A box coat was hanging from a peg.

He tossed another pebble at the siding, waited for the count of ten, proceeded to the window. From here he had a clear view of a spinning wheel upended in a corner, chips of earthenware, a shattered armchair . . . perhaps dried blood . . .

The arrangement of bloodstains suggested that there had been two occupants, and the bodies were now in the keeping room where they had been tossed. The first, an elderly man, had been shot while seated in the chair. The second, a girl, had been clubbed, then her throat cut. The man had been thrown against a far wall. The girl was partially entangled in his arms.

The occupants disposed of, Dawes had then prepared himself for the task at hand . . . by the window adjacent to the door was a spyglass, sticks of dried beef and three long-barrelled rifles. There were also twists of that Jamestown weed. Given the distance and angle of the shore, Grove supposed that the thing was to be done when the general's barge neared the rocks to navigate a bend. Those Tories on the opposite banks—men with musket and mortar, would drive the barge closer, where even a modest rifleman couldn't miss.

As for Dawes' whereabouts at the moment, Grove figured he had either moved to the high ground for a broader view of the river, or else was exploring the low ground to determine his escape.

Either way, he would be back.

He crouched in the corner to the left of the door. At first even a breath of wind sent his right hand to the pistol beside him, but after a while he almost welcomed such distractions, along with the rustling of leaves and scurrying of mice in the thatch. Although he had no view of the sky the lengthening shadow of a chair told him that the sun was nearly below the hills.

He worried about his position relative to the entrance, the angle and thickness of the door. Also about having left footprints on the path, and about his horse still unfettered out there among the elms. He felt a strong thirst, knew it was fear, and then was aware of nothing except the sound of approaching footsteps on the path.

chapter
thirty-six

Grove lifted the pistol slowly, bracing the arm on a knee, his shoulder to the wainscot. The room was dark by now and the breeze had grown stronger. The footsteps, however, punctuated by the sound of the man's breath, were unmistakable. The man's walk was lithe, not unlike an Iroquois', or even some animal a savage might imitate.

The man hesitated at the step, then again at the door, and Grove wondered if that Jamestown weed didn't also create an uncommon ability to sense danger.

But then came the hand on the latch, a glimpse of sleeve, and a boot on the floorboards.

Grove waited until both boots sounded on the floorboards.

Then, aiming for what he supposed was Dawes' chest, pulled the trigger.

No cry of pain, no stumbling footsteps . . . only a shadow rebounding off the wall. And then gone.

But there was blood on the jamb, more in the splintered wood where the ball had passed clean through the door.

Grove reloaded the first pistol, peered out into near darkness. Did he detect something beginning to sway among the swamp grass?

I'll give him an hour, Grove told himself. Give him an hour and let him bleed to death. But even as the thought formed he knew that it was empty.

He replaced the second pistol in his belt and moved out in a low crouch to the first rank of oaks. There were more clumps of timothy here, clover and what could have been blood among the trampled ferns. A muskrat slid into the deeper vegetation. Then, plainly, from the rise—another footstep on dry leaves.

Grove sank to a knee, once more bracing the pistol on it.

Then from a circle of elms at forty paces—Dawes again with what must have been a carbine.

Grove shot for the belly, squeezing his whole hand, not just the finger. He felt a ball graze his shoulder, but his own shot must have been square—a gut shot that briefly left Dawes motionless before tossing him into the reeds.

Yet when he moved to that circle of elms he once more found only hints of the man—a line of bootprints into the hollows, crushed leaves, and more blood.

He sat now, examining his shoulder. It seemed the ball had only sliced the flesh—what Dr. Rush would call an honorable wound—but there was still a fair amount of bleeding and throbbing pain from the elbow.

He shut his eyes, briefly remembering Dawes collapsing into the reeds. He glanced at what must have been another bootprint along the sandy bank. *They were right, he's not human.* He got to his feet. *He's a damn werewolf.* Or, more to the point, has learned to ignore pain.

Below the knoll the bootprints grew deeper, indicating a lagging step. There was also more blood here—a lot of it smeared on the trunk of an elm. Beyond the elms the ground rose sharply to another wooded glade of snake vines, creepers and thistle, then fell again to an incline of rocks along the water.

At first when he was approaching this glade he figured his quarry had been crippled, else why would he have fled to the low ground? But once he was beyond the second rank of elms a very different possisbility took over—a direct confrontation on the high ground.

There was another deer path here, a narrow ribbon of sandy ground littered with fallen debris from the elms. At some forty paces he discarded his coat and horn. At thirty he let the pistol slip from his hand and took out his dagger.

Dawes seemed to hesitate a moment before moving into the clearing. Bleeding heavily, he showed no pain. His eyes were fixed on nothing Grove could see. Then his left hand discarded his empty carbine, and the right emerged from his tunic—holding that mason's trowel, still chipped but otherwise lethal.

They closed on one another slowly, circling clockwise, then briefly merging to become a single shadow. When they parted again a new line of blood had appeared on Dawes' left cheek.

Feinting for the groin, Grove twisted in midstep and nearly severed Dawes' ear. Dawes seemed not to notice. Did he actually grin?

Dawes began to circle again, and Grove wondered what if anything could stop this man. Cut him like a pig? Cut out the tongue? Take his cue and pack the mouth with lime and sand? Or meet him head on . . . full force?

There was another moment when Grove simply looked at the

251

man, and looked at him, thinking: *There, you can feel me now, can't you? Right there at the back of the throat. And yes, we're not so different, are we? Born a couple of centuries too soon, and not much liking it.*

To hell with thinking. He struck, this time not feinting but head on, full force, still holding the gaze. He saw the eyes widen as the throat released a rush of blood. He felt the hand shuddering on his wrist, and in spite of himself wondered if there had been this perverse sort of intimacy at the White Swan.

Stepping back, he watched as Dawes crumpled—first to one knee, then to the other, then slowly deeper into the leaves. He watched as the lips attempted to form a word. *You? Me?* Then, although the fingers may have closed around the handle of the trowel, the rest of the man was clearly dead.

chapter
thirty-seven

There was talk that the White Swan killer was to be put on public display, but nothing of the sort was actually done. Instead the corpse was carried to Tappan and buried. The weapons, including the infamous trowel, were disposed of without ceremony. Nor was there any celebration . . . the people's spirits continued to remain low in the wake of the Benedict Arnold affair.

Given the demands that the Arnold revelation put on Tallmadge, it was not until late Thursday that he and Grove were able to return to the White Swan business, and even then there was much to blacken the moment, what with the pending execution of John André.

The Traitor

Their meeting took place in a potter's field between the Old Tappan Road and the King's Highway. Grove had arrived exhausted, and still bleeding slightly. Tallmadge was sitting on a low stone wall.

Their conversation began with the plight of young André. Although his fate had not yet been formally sealed there seemed little doubt he would hang by the following Monday or Tuesday. To make matters worse he had turned out to be a likeable fellow. Even his worst opponents had been touched by him. He'd not complained about his fate nor in any way compromised his integrity as an officer. He admitted his guilt and said his captors had the right to execute him. He was even polite to his guards.

"He's a victim," Tallmadge was saying.

"Then petition the damn Congress," Grove said. "Or speak to the general."

Tallmadge turned to face him. "Speak to him yourself."

Although considered an imposing man—rank defined status—on this evening General Washington's face was deathly white, he had a slight limp, his wig askew. His cloak, like Grove's, had been badly soiled from the road. His boots needed cleaning. As he approached, Grove moved slowly out across the field to meet him. Tallmadge stayed behind.

Grove hardly saluted, said only, "Your Excellency."

Washington nodded. "They tell me you were wounded, sir."

"Hardly."

"Still, even a minor cut can turn sour in this weather."

Grove's eyes once more swept this ugly little field. He withdrew his papers then—three scrawled-on pages accounting for the death of Corporal Dawes.

Washington accepted them without a glance, then said, "You've done us a great service, and here I've forgotten to congratulate you, much less reward you."

Grove looked directly at him. "I think, sir, you know what I want."

"Yes, I think I do. However, I'm told that we can't rely on anyone's testimony in this matter, not even Miss Claire's. I'm also told, Mr. Grove, that a public prosecution would only alienate certain parties to whom we are indebted on account of their ships, their money and their influence . . . and so it seems that for the sake of our cause a bargain is more expedient than a hanging. I'm sure this gives you no comfort, but—"

"I appreciate your confidences, sir, but it's not my intention to see the man hanged . . ."

"No, you only want to see him dead."

"And you, sir?"

The sound of distant wagons, a train of cannon that might have been part of Edwin Hyde's bargain, Grove thought.

"Mr. Grove, I do not have the luxury of self-indulgence. I have a responsibility, and I am responsible—"

"To whom?"

"To our Congress."

"Then what's the point of hanging John André?"

The thumb and foreginger pressed to the eyes. "Mr. Tallmadge understands these things . . . I'm told the people expect it."

They began to walk, following the wall, the general's limp more pronounced now so that an observer might have thought him wounded.

"And," Washington said abruptly, "there's one's own allegiance to consider. I can't ask or expect you to appreciate my feelings, you're not part of the Order . . ."

"If you'll forgive me, sir, I can't imagine—"

"Exactly, Mr. Grove. You can't imagine. But I tell you . . . you're entitled to an explanation . . . that the Brotherhood has made a great contribution to our cause. Regardless of what

Hyde and his conspirators may have done, it mustn't be forgotten that this Revolution would have failed long ago were it not sustained by the Brotherhood—"

"But Hyde is a traitor. He has—"

"Hyde is not a true Brother, Mr. Grove. He's a pretender, a pretender and a usurper. But I can't destroy him if it means losing the support of the Order. Support we so badly need to prevail." He looked unhappily at Grove. "I'm sorry, Mr. Grove, and I can hardly blame you for the anger and frustration you are undoubtedly now feeling."

When Grove said nothing, the general seemed compelled to explain further. "Mr. Grove, the Order is no ordinary fraternity, or gaggle of merchants plotting in the darkness. It's more a college, a vast college of like minds working in many places and many ways to improve this world. I believe one day people will recognize that our nation was at least partially forged by Masons."

They had reached the end of the field, with a view of the Mablie Tavern, where André had been confined since the previous Tuesday. "Benjamin tells me that you've become quite taken with Miss Claire. Is that true, Mr. Grove?"

Grove did not respond.

"Not that I blame you. She is, after all, an extremely attractive woman. Unfortunately, she is still, so to speak, Mr. Hyde's property, and I doubt he will give her up without a struggle."

Grove wanted to hit somebody.

"So we seem to have a problem. You want to set the woman free, Hyde wants to keep her, to possess her." Grove's whole body stiffened. "So what are we to do, Mr. Grove?"

"General, with respect, I hardly see—"

"Don't you? I think it's clear. I have been advised that no official" . . . he delicately underlined the word . . . "action may be taken against Mr. Hyde for fear of upsetting a political apple cart and embarrassing my fellows. You, on the other hand, have a legitimate grievance with the man that has nothing whatever to do with politics. So I put it to you once again, what are we to do?"

Did he, Grove wondered, detect a nod, the suggestion of a smile? He would test it . . . "Where is he? Hyde?"

"At his eastern estate . . . soon, I'm told, bound for Montreal, a part of the bargain, I believe."

"And he is alone?"

"Mr. Grove . . ."

"You would have no objection if—"

"Mr. Grove, how can I object to something I know nothing about, to something that was never discussed?" They had reached the wooden gate that served as an entrance to the field. "And by the way, Mr. Grove, if I'm not mistaken your shoulder is bleeding again. You should see the good Dr. Rush."

Grove had, finally, the sense to hold his tongue.

Grove set out shortly before dawn of Friday. The special board of inquiry that would condemn André was soon to convene. There was still much talk about Arnold, and news of the White Swan killer had spread.

None of these were on Matty Grove's mind as he spent the first night in the saddle, the second in a wayside inn where they may not have been certain who he was but they nonetheless kept their distance.

chapter
thirty-eight

Approached from the north, Hyde's estate could first be
sighted from a distance of about two miles. As the road plunged
into a copse of dark oaks one lost sight of it until again mounting
the hill, from which the estate seemed to rise up suddenly like a
giant.

The house was an imposing structure—five bays wide and
symmetrical, constructed according to the precepts of Inigo
Jones: "Solid, masculine, and proportionable according to rule."
The windows were capped with segmented arches, one on top of
the other.

* * *

Hyde first saw Grove approaching from a second-floor window. He called for a servant, before he remembered there were no servants about. Descending to what had been his drawing room, he poured himself a drink and sat down.

Which was how Grove found him, seated among tortoiseshell shadows, somewhat drunk from the whiskey poured from a decanter sitting on a circular table. Like the other lower rooms, this one was nearly bare: walls stripped of furnishings, rugs removed, shutters nailed fast.

"Miss Claire and I made a wager," Hyde said. "Seven English pounds. She maintained that hell would freeze over before you actually set foot in this house. I, on the other hand, maintained that you would appear within the week. I wonder, do you think she'll actually pay up?"

Grove moved from the doorway across the bare floor, tossed his cloak aside to reveal his pistols—the left loaded with shot, the right with a single ball. "Where is she?"

Hyde nodded to the staircase. "Upstairs, packing, for our honorable retreat, so to speak, to the bracing climes of Montreal. Tell me, do you feel victorious, Mr. Grove? Are you so deceived?"

"I want to see her," was Grove's only answer.

"And so you shall . . . but first I was looking forward to a private chat." He stood, poured a second glass. "Really, what two men could have more in common than you and I? After all, we have lived in one another's imagination from the start of this business. I as your quarry, you as my hunter. Not even lovers can claim that sort of intimacy."

There was the double click of a shutting door, then a footstep on the floorboards above.

"She's not going with you, Hyde. She's staying—"

"And that's another thing. We've even shared the same woman."

Another step on the floorboards above, hesitant. Hyde either didn't hear it or chose to ignore it.

"Indeed, it would seem that the only difference between us, Mr. Grove, is that while you represent an empty, discredited and, forgive me, naive past, I represent the future. Which is what the Freemasons are about . . . shaping the future with an ancient wisdom."

He moved to the window, looked out into the yard at two wagons laden with household goods and at a third whose axle had broken under the weight of furniture, then turned to face Grove. "There will always be soldiers like yourself, Mr. Grove, to conquer and die, but I think the world will be run by people like me." He tossed back the remainder of the whiskey. "By the way, that's why General Washington decided to spare himself, and me, the inconvenience of a trial. He may be a fool in many respects, but at least he knows which side of the bread has to be buttered." He smiled, apparently pleased with his turn of phrase.

By now the footsteps had passed from the room above to an empty passage. She was still, however, afraid to move down the staircase.

Hyde continued suddenly, "You still haven't told me how you managed to kill my White Swan phantom."

Grove moved back to the doorway in hopes of glimpsing her on the landing. There was no one.

"You know, in many ways," Hyde went on, "Dawes was my most ingenious piece of work—an archetypal monster, a wonderfully ancient and terrible beast that had the whole countryside terrified . . . not to mention my occasionally wayward Brethren of the Lodge. And how he obeyed. A fine student. Pity I was never able to instill such loyalty and fervor in Miss Claire . . . Tell me something, Mr. Grove. If it weren't that I'm still able to influence the importation of powder from abroad and so still hold importance to your cause, would I be dead by now?

Would you have already put a ball into my heart? Come now, be honest. Wouldn't you have already put a ball into my heart?"

Grove shook his head.

"No, Mr. Hyde. I'd have put the ball right there," pointing to the bridge of his nose. "Now tell her to come downstairs."

Hyde refilled his glass, sank back into the chair and shut his eyes. "Did she happen to mention that I've had her for a very long time? And if you think she's exquisite now, you should have seen her at age ten, naked, prostrate at my feet, crying out her little heart. Of course I only played with her until she reached the age of twelve, and trained her in anticipation. But such perfection. You really can't imagine such *unholy* perfection."

Grove's fists clenched. "Tell her to come downstairs."

"I suppose that's why she can't leave me now. I created her, I put part of my own soul into her. She'll always carry something of me inside of her . . ."

"Tell her, damn you, to come down or I'll—"

"There's no need," she said from the doorway.

She had taken off her shoes, which accounted for her silence on the staircase. The rest of her was as expected. Her hair, unbound, fell in ringlets to her shoulders. Her dress, secured at the waist with a broad sash, made her look a little like a shepherdess.

"Now, doesn't that exemplify her beauty? Even in this peasant dress she's still incomparable."

Grove moved to her, held out a hand. She shook her head.

"There, you see, Mr. Grove. If nothing else the lady knows her master. Now tell him, Nancy dear, tell him why you will always belong to me, with me . . . Here, I'll make it easy for you. I shall make it *painfully* easy for both of you," and reaching into the pocket of his coat he brought out her tiny inlaid pistol—her so-called last resort. *"Voilà.* I lay it on the table . . . Now my darling, pick it up. You see, Mr. Grove is bound by honor and the needs of his cause to restrain himself from harming me. So the task falls on your shoulders, my dear. Collect your weapon and shoot me. Come on, if you want this man so badly, then shoot me."

All she managed was to look briefly at Grove, then away.

"There, now you've seen it for yourself, Mr. Grove. You've seen it for yourself—still a child, still mine for life. Now, Mr. Grove, get out. Get out of what's left of my house—"

She had lunged for the table, scooped up the pistol and squeezed the trigger.

"*Click.*" Hyde smiled. Again the hammer fell on an empty pan. "*Click, click . . .* I'm not a fool, my dear. And I'm impressed by your spirit . . . it seems I did an even better job than I'd thought. Well, you're better than a mere possession, which makes me even more determined to keep you."

The pistol hung limp in her hand now as Hyde moved toward her. "Bitch . . . whore . . ." and as his arm rose to strike her, Grove at last withdrew his own pistol.

He fired from the hip, aiming, as he'd promised, for the bridge of Hyde's nose. Actually the ball entered above the left eye, leaving a black hole, then a larger circle of blood. Hyde stiffened before he fell, a look of disbelief still on his face.

Grove came to her slowly, first taking the little pistol from her hand, then kneeling to place it in Hyde's lifeless hand. Not that the man's wound exactly suggested suicide, but he at least owed himself—and the general—protection from another charge of murder.

epilogue

The effect of Edwin Hyde's death on the Revolution occupied a number of minds through the trailing days of October. There were those, Mr. Robert Morris in particular, who claimed that Hyde's death would cause irreparable harm to the new nation's credibility abroad and might lengthen hostilities by at least a year. Others, specifically Mr. Jefferson, maintained that such fears were nonsense, that the success of this cause was dependent on all citizens, not to be undone by any single traitor. If Edwin Hyde had been guilty of treason, then let him be damned to hell.

Among lesser figures, those at the Dwarf, for example, the judgments were less dramatic. Apart from a minor incident involving young Sarah, hardly anyone even talked about the White

263

Epilogue

Swan affair much beyond November. But since Sarah Dunn's finish would bring this story full circle, so to speak, it bears repeating . . .

One afternoon shortly after Matty Grove left the city in the company of Miss Claire, Sarah was tending to her chores when she noticed the approach of a fair-haired boy in the uniform of a Continental soldier. His age, she guessed, was about eighteen. His rank, judging from the condition of his tunic, was low. Nonetheless he was handsome enough, with a spray of oak leaves in his hat and a blunderbuss across his shoulder. Although she at first exchanged only a lingering glance with the boy as he entered the Dwarf to secure his lodgings, it wasn't long before he confided his story.

His name was Tommy Finch, he said, which generally struck a chord in folks since he was the same Thomas Finch who had first discovered those bodies at the White Swan. He said that most people usually made for the door when he told them who he was on account of the fact that the sight of those bodies was supposed to have driven him mad. But he was not mad, and the sight of those bodies had, as it turned out, only driven him to adventure.

At the start of his soldiering career he had served with General Greene as a drummer and occasional surgeon's mate. But owing to the shortage of men they finally gave him a blunderbuss to shoot whatever Redcoats happened to cross his path.

And shoot them he did—first at Morristown, then at Springfield, then at the Vauxhall Bridge. Between these battles he had, he said, seen some strange and wonderous sights. Like an Indian chief with at least twenty scalps attached to his belt, and a giant woodsman with a blade on his axe the size of a mule's head. Also, he said, warming to his audience, a pirate from New Orleans and the ghost of a beheaded piper. He had even seen Major André mount the scaffold and whisper, " 'Tis but a momentary pang."

Yet for all these wondrous sights and adventures there was

264

still one thing that young Finch very much wanted to do; he wanted to tip his hat to Mr. Matty Grove and thank him for having killed the White Swan fiend.

"Ah," Sarah sighed, "if only you had come a month or two earlier then surely such a thing could have been arranged." As it stood now, she said that Matty Grove was long gone and no one knew where he had gone.

Finch now grew quiet. Then suddenly taking Sarah's hand, he asked if he couldn't at least see the room where Grove had lived.

Of course he could see the room, Sarah told him, and still holding his hand, led him to that oblong chamber above the carriage yard.

Although this chamber no longer showed any tangible signs of the man, nothing had really changed. There, for example, was where Mr. Grove had taken his meals, Sarah said, pointing to the table in the corner. And there was where he occasionally slept . . . and here was where he paced the floor . . .

She did not include in her tour for young Finch the window from which she had watched Mr. Grove rush off to that woman, the one he was said to have now gone off with after the death of some man named Hyde. Nor did she allow Finch to enter her feelings, deep within which she would always have a place for Mr. Matty Grove.